Banshee Power

Blood Fae Chronicles
Book 3

USA TODAY BEST SELLING AUTHOR
JEN KATEMI

Contents

Chapter One

MAEWEN

I've been staring at this damn enchanted medallion for so long, my eyes are getting blurry. The new vamp police sergeant in our team, Luc Durand, handed it over to me after the abomination attack in Hatton Grove, and I've been studying it in my spare moments, trying to figure out how to unlock its secrets.

It is definitely infused with necromancer magic, and interestingly, fae magic, too. Our calibration meter —the only one of its kind in the world designed to identify the source of magic trace—has ascertained that much. Beyond that little snippet, the medallion has frustratingly managed to keep its mysteries undiscovered.

The design, though, matches what we found on a bracelet beside a dead necromancer last week. The guy was discovered in a back alley in the northern part of the city, lying half-melted in a puddle of stinking pus that had leached from his body. He'd clearly died of some kind of poisoning. The reason my team was called in, as well as the standard city police, was because someone noticed the purple trace still swirling around the bracelet.

Eventually the piece of jewelry found its way here to the lab, and our trusty calibration meter established what kind of magic it contained.

The same unusual combination of magics as the medallion.

Necros and fae do not often collaborate. They certainly do not collaborate with supernatural creatures turned loup.

Is that how the rogue supes attacking humans are being controlled? By a necromancer "pilot", who is being assisted behind the scenes by a fae?

Yet another night is almost over, and there are still no concrete answers as to how the supernatural abominations are being controlled, nor why. Nor even *who* is behind the chaos and the violent deaths.

I glance at my watch and discover that it is almost midnight. Where does the time go? I need to finish up and head home, before I fall asleep right here, slumped on the work bench of SUDAP's police lab in Melbourne.

The fifteen-strong members of my team already left earlier in the evening. They are generally a good bunch, accepting of having a female as their officer-in-charge. Most nights at least some of us will stay back late, depending on who caught what case, and where we're at in our various investigations, but I am often the last one out the door each night.

I love my job as an inspector in Australia's first national police Supernatural Division, but even I know that sometimes, I can be a little obsessive over cases that pique my interest.

I expect dedication from my team, but I don't believe in working them so hard they burn out. *No, you're leaving that fate for yourself*, my traitorous inner voice whispers.

As usual, I ignore my inner voice. She's far too annoying. Though I have to admit I am more tired than I should be, tonight. The nightmares are getting worse. I don't know how much longer I can keep tamping down my magic.

I twirl the silver ring on the little finger of my right hand. It is set with a multi-colored opal infused with a charm.

I purchased the ring from a witch mage I met during a case several years ago. The power it has been imbued with, has enabled me to work as a police officer without curling up in an agonized ball of tears and snot every time a death takes place.

The mage warned me there would be consequences, but I didn't realize quite how debilitating it would be to have the little sleep I do manage to get filled constantly with nightmares of death and dying.

As I place the medallion back in a reinforced glass cabinet in the lab, and peel off my protective gloves and face shield, a giant yawn almost splits my face in two. Definitely time for bed.

After I lock up the lab, the small lamp in my corner office is the only illumination left on the whole floor. I head through the open-plan area where the team sits, back toward my desk. I make a mental note to ask the cleaning staff to keep the hall lights on from now on, and allow me to turn them off when I leave. No wonder my eyes are getting wonky.

I wriggle my shoulders and crick my neck, and my stomach gives a loud rumble to remind me I need sustenance. I don't think I've eaten since breakfast this morning. *Well...* I glance again at my watch and amend my thoughts. *Yesterday* morning.

Luckily there's a twenty-four-hour pizza place almost next door to my apartment building a few blocks from here, so I can pick up some take-out on the way home.

As I grab my bag from the corner of the room and lean over the desk to switch off the lamp, a flash of silver light brightens the space. What the heck? I blink fast, trying to recover my vision as I scrabble for the gun on my belt. Silver light usually means fae, and there is no one of that species on my team.

Two tall, dark-haired men materialize in the room.

Definitely fae. Specifically, it is the fae warrior I met briefly several days ago—Tarrien, his name was— at the cabaret club when the singer Indigo was snatched. He is accompanied by another fae, almost a head taller than Tarrien. Quite impressive, given Tarrien is over six feet tall. I've never met the second fae before.

I point my gun at the second man's chest before either man tries to greet me.

"Who the hell are you?" I ask. "And what do you want?"

"Inspector Jones, please." Tarrien shakes his head, reproach in his tone. "That's no way to greet royalty."

Royalty? The other fae inclines his head gracefully and then studies me, as if waiting for something. Does he expect me to bow? Curtsy? Fall at his feet in supplication?

He'll be waiting a damn long time, if that's the case.

Instead, I simply raise a brow.

To be honest, it's a bit hard to ignore how handsome the second man is, and how much he actually does give off the air of being someone rather important. There's a magnetic charisma that draws me toward him. Of the two visitors, the taller one is definitely the more commanding. I plant my feet firmly, refusing to give in to the impulse.

Eventually the taller fae scowls and folds his arms across his chest.

Tarrien gestures. "Inspector Maewen Jones, meet your prince, His Royal Highness, Prince Rhodri, of the Winter Court of Faerie."

My prince? I don't think so. I cock the hammer on the gun, enjoying the faint flicker of shock on the prince's face a little too much. *Careful, Maewen. You're over-tired. Don't play with guns. Don't tease the royal guy.*

Bet most of his subjects kowtow to him. I can't imagine many point a gun.

A gun that shoots a special type of bullet comprising a mix of silver and iron. The prince of winter would not enjoy it, should my trigger finger spasm.

Slowly I re-engage the safety and re-holster the weapon.

The wariness in both Prince Rhodri's expression, and Tarrien's, reduces a notch.

"Pleasure to meet you, gents," I say. "But you haven't answered the second part of my question. What do you want? And please, make it quick. I'm hungry, and I'm tired, and I don't have an ounce of patience left in my body or my soul, tonight."

Tarrien sighs, more dramatically than I think is warranted.

"What is it about Renna's children?" he murmurs as if to himself.

The mention of my banshee mother causes a shard of annoyance in my chest. I resist the impulse to roll my eyes.

The fae prince chuckles.

"As you are probably aware, Tarrien is dating your half-sister," Rhodri says. When he speaks, he looks directly at me, making me feel as if his full attention is on me. The courtesy is strangely attractive. "And I believe Indigo does not always do what Tarrien wants, nor expects."

Tarrien shuffles his feet and picks at the edge of his jacket during the prince's explanation. A grin hovers about my lips. *Well, well. Good for you, Indigo.*

"I can answer your other query, Inspector Maewen Jones," Prince Rhodri continues.

I want to tell him it's Inspector Jones, or even just Boss, as many of the team call me. But what comes out of my mouth instead is, "Maewen. Call me Maewen, sir."

Hell. Where did that come from?

The prince smiles—one of those rare ones that actually reaches the eyes. Most people don't smile with their eyes, at least in my experience. I draw in a quick breath, trying to steady myself. His effect on my senses is completely unexpected.

"Maewen," he repeats. "Such a lovely name. I insist that you call me Rhodri in return. You want to know why we're here, Maewen? We're here because of this."

He gestures to Tarrien, who pulls a plastic packet from a previously hidden inner pocket in his coat and thrusts it in my direction.

"I found this on a loup werewolf," Tarrien says. "In

the Badlands, on the edge of Faerie. That's where they were holding Indie. There was a whole conclave of necromancers there. Wizards, a couple of witches, and a slew of rogue supes, all gowned up and readying for some kind of ritual that involved draining your sister of her banshee blood."

Slowly, I take the packet from him.

"She's fine by the way," he adds. "Thanks for asking."

I bite back a growl of annoyance. "I *know*, Tarrien. Indigo called me several hours ago and we had quite a long chat. She wants to meet in person soon, and I have agreed to that."

"Oh."

A small sound from the prince catches my attention and I see him biting back a grin.

The urge to grin with him rises. I manage to restrain the impulse, and return to study the packet's contents. It is half-wrapped in a handkerchief, within the plastic packet, but the shape of it is obvious.

"Another medallion?" I shoot them a glance, excitement punching me in the gut. Maybe this one will be easier to crack. Then a thought strikes and I frown up at Tarrien. "Did you touch it?"

"No. I used the linen handkerchief to pull it off the dead were, and then sealed it straight into the plastic. It felt...wrong, when I saw it, so I instinctively avoided touching it."

"Good." Gut instinct tells me these medallions are

bad news, and I suspect things might bode badly for anyone who happens to touch one without a protective layer between. "Until we have more information about how they work, best not to touch them directly."

Prince Rhodri steps up beside me then, and stares down at the packet in my hand. His body imparts a pleasant warmth, creating an unexpected—and definitely unwanted—shiver down my spine.

Surreptitiously, I slide away. The prince is no fool, though. He flashes me a knowing grin. The man is too astute for my liking.

"Thank you for bringing this to SUDAP," I say. "I'll need to lock it away with the other talismans for now, and get the team onto it tomorrow. Hopefully we'll manage to extract some answers from them, soon enough."

"Would it help if you know who made them?" Prince Rhodri leans against the edge of my desk, making himself at home. He looks most un-royal-like. In his casual street clothing of dark jeans with heavy boots, a white tee-shirt and black leather jacket, he could pass for an extremely charismatic human male. Except for those pointed ears that show when he tosses back his long hair, and the aristocratic line of his nose, and those chiselled high cheekbones above the sexy-as-fuck mouth. And of course, the amazing, brilliant blue eyes that remind me of the sky on a sunny winter's day...

Jesus. I shake my head. What the hell is wrong with

me, tonight?

"It might," I answer carefully. "*Do* you know who created them?"

Tarrien clears his throat. When I transfer my attention to him, his mouth tightens in a grim line and his eyes are flat and steely in color. "I believe it was my father."

Wait. What?

"Your father is responsible for these medallions? But...that means he's responsible for..." *All the carnage.* I can't finish the sentence out loud. The disclosure is as unexpected as it is horrifying. The trail of violence and death caused by the rogue supes is long and bloody, enacted over many years. I might have a deep personal dislike of the banshee woman who birthed me and then flitted off to live her life without me, but I can't imagine what it would be like knowing one of your parents was responsible for so much suffering and death.

Before I can ask *why*, Prince Rhodri speaks up, as if sensing that Tarrien isn't in the mood to admit anything further. "We believe Tarrien's father created the medallions with the help of a group of necromancers, and somehow they are using those to turn supernaturals loup and then control them.

"But he only did that, because he is working for my mother, formerly Queen Rhiannon of the Winter

Court. She was banished from Faerie more than twenty-five years ago." Rhodri's gaze hardens, the bright blue of his eyes turning stormy. "It is my belief that every action she undertakes is designed as part of a long-game, to try and take the throne from my father."

My mouth drops open and stays like that for a few seconds too long. Eventually, I realize I'm gaping. *Holy hell. We're going up against a queen of Faerie?*

To give myself time to process what Rhodri has just said, I make my way around the desk and flop down into my chair, leaning back and steepling my fingers in front of my lips.

"That is a lot to take in," I manage, at last. "I assumed we maybe had a mad necromancer or two on our hands. A small group at most. This pushes the issue into a whole other level of concerning."

Rhodri nods, and leans forward over the desk, piercing me with his steady gaze. "We wish to join forces with you and your SUDAP team, Maewen."

He thumps the top of the wooden desk surface with a fist and I jump at the sharp and unexpected sound.

"Let us share our information, and help each other," he says. "That will provide the best chance of locating Rhiannon and Tarrien's father, Targon."

I stare up at Rhodri, unable to tear my gaze away from his intense scrutiny.

"And then?" I ask.

His eyes light up with a fierce blue glow, so bright I have to blink several times to avoid being temporarily blinded.

"And then, Maewen," he says, "we are going to kill them."

Chapter Two

RHODRI

I did not expect Lady Renna's daughter to be so interesting. The way Tarrien described her, as a hard-nosed and uncompromising police officer without a humorous bone in her body, had me imagining someone completely different to the obviously intelligent and very sexy half-banshee who faced us in her office.

How does she do her job, surrounded by death? How does she balance the banshee power that swirls within her, with her human duties as an officer of the law? Banshee magic is part of Winter Faerie and as such, we are already connected, even though I could not sense anything in her while standing in her office.

Tiredness was evident in the tightness of her skin around those large hazel-colored eyes, and in the faint lines each side of her beautiful mouth. I cannot imagine the agony of what she must go through every time her team catches a murder case. Perhaps it drains her, and her magic takes time to replenish?

Inspector Maewen Jones is an enigma. I am glad she has agreed to pool our resources and work together. I have the feeling it is better to have someone like Maewen *on* our side, than against us.

It is frustrating that she needs to head home and sleep, but she is half-human, after all. I guess she does not have the stamina of a full fae like myself or Tarrien.

"Look, I need to go home, and I need to eat," she says. "Why don't you guys join me? We can eat pizza while we talk."

Her offer is a generous one, though *pizza* is not something I have ever eaten before so I am not sure about that part of the invitation.

"I'll have to sign out a vehicle from the fleet, gents," she says. "Don't think you'll both fit on the back of my motorbike. It's only a few blocks, but I'm not walking it at this time of night."

I laugh and show her the filigree ring on my thumb. Tarrien has a similar one; in fact, all Winter fae wear one.

"We can meet you there," I say. "Fae, remember? We raise a portal, and we jump. Would you like to accompany us down the faerie paths? It will be quicker than your motorbike."

Maewen's eyes narrow.

"I'll meet you there," she says, and reels off an

address. "At the front door, please. Don't go inside my apartment without me."

I am not used to being ordered around by anyone. At first, her tone annoys me. But then I decide to shrug it off. Maybe it is the way of humans, to have less respect for their leaders? I do not spend long periods of time in the human realm, though I have been here often, of course. Many of the Winter Court's subjects have permanent homes in realms other than Faerie, and it is my duty as the heir apparent to understand as much as I can about all worlds in which our subjects reside, not just my own.

That task has become even more important, since the Accord was struck thirty-odd years ago. Winter fae became a party to the Accord when my father, the king, signed the Agreement. We need to remain as informed as we can about happenings everywhere. Unfortunately, my father is not as capable as he once was. Things changed when Mother was banished, and over time, the task has fallen to me, to keep an eye on the various realms.

Perhaps I should start extending my visits to the human realm from now on. Especially if there are creatures as intriguing as Inspector Maewen Jones to pique my interest along the way.

True to her word, Maewen meets us at the entrance to her apartment. She carries two large flat cardboard boxes in her arms, from which a delicious smell rises.

Is that pizza? How have I not tried this delicacy, before now?

"Hey boys, come on in. Welcome to my humble abode."

She balances the boxes on one arm and leads the way inside a very small suite of rooms. In fact, it can hardly be called a suite. There is only one room, as far as I can tell, that doubles as both living and sleeping area. There is a food preparation area in one corner, two compact sofas divided by a coffee table in the middle, and a large bed and chest of drawers in the opposite corner. A fold-out screen separates the bed from the rest. There appears to be a bathing room off to one side, but that's it. The space is neat enough, but it is hardly cozy or homely.

Humble is the right word. Do all police officers have so little in this realm? Our warriors in Faerie are treated much more generously than this. Most have large suites within the royal palace, as well as the opportunity for multiple homes wherever they wish to set them up.

"Take a seat, and dig in," Maewen says, setting the boxes on a small table by the couch. "I'll be with you in a sec."

She disappears into the bathroom, presumably to freshen herself up, or perhaps to remove her gun belt and stow it safely away. I follow Tarrien's example and sit beside him on one of the two sofa couches, leaving the other for our host when she returns. Tarrien opens the boxes and removes a slice of flat pie, so I do the same.

The taste when it hits my mouth is divine. Hot and spicy and full of grease, which should turn my stomach but instead, is quite delicious.

When Maewen returns, my mouth is full so I give her a greasy thumbs up. She flashes me a surprised grin, and my pulse rate jumps unexpectedly. When she smiles in a genuine way, her whole face lights up.

She should smile like that, more often.

Maewen sits opposite us and carefully places her mobile phone on the table in front of her. Only then does she grab some pizza for herself. Once she has eaten three slices, she wipes her mouth and fingers on a paper napkin and sits back with a satisfied sigh. "Oh, I needed that. Now, how shall we do this? Do you want to go first, Rhodri, and share what you know?"

I also wipe the grease away with a napkin, and lean back. "Ladies first."

"Hmm. Well, I'm not a lady, so nope. Royalty should go first."

"Oh, no. I insist."

"No, *I* insist. You're my guest."

We lock eyes in what feels like an unwinnable glaring match, until Tarrien huffs out a breath.

"For the love of the winter gods, *I'll* go first."

He proceeds to provide a summary to Maewen— and to me, as I haven't yet heard the full story—about what happened when Indie was held captive in the Badlands.

The poor girl. It must have been terrifying for her to be kept immobile by magic, helpless and unmoving, and believing she was about to be murdered in such a heinous manner.

Shame fills me. Shame that I carry the exiled queen's tainted blood in my veins. Shame that my father, the king himself, has been so caught up in his internal grief at banishing the woman he loved—that he perhaps *still* loves—that he has been unable to perceive the growing threat. Or perhaps he *has* seen it, and chooses not to do anything about it.

I am not my parents, I remind myself.

I have free will to choose my own path.

While Tarrien speaks, Maewen sits forward, listening intently, and I have the opportunity to study her in more depth. At first glance, there is a definite surface brashness, and yet I suspect that may be a front. Every so often her guard drops and I catch a glimpse of something else in her expression. Something sad and haunting and indescribably lonely.

The need to take her in my arms and hold her, not for sexual gratification but simply to comfort her, grows. I shift in my seat, unused to such strange impulses. Sex to a fae is as natural as breathing, and while there is definitely an element of sexual attraction to the banshee sitting across from me, it feels like there is something else layered over the top of that desire.

Something that does not lend itself to any kind of label I'm familiar with.

Lost in my musings, I realize Tarrien has finished speaking.

"And, Indigo is all right?" Maewen asks. "I mean, I know she's safe, physically. But...mentally?"

"Yes, she's incredibly strong and resilient," Tarrien answers.

Again, there's a glimpse of vulnerability in Maewen, just for a moment. She might pretend to be disinterested in her banshee family, but she is obviously relieved to hear that Indie is okay. As am I.

She shoots a glance at me, as if uncomfortable with my keen regard. I turn my attention back to Tarrien, to allow her a moment to gather herself.

"Indie is back here at her apartment in the human realm. Lady Renna accompanied her." His expression turns fierce. "I have ensured her home and her workplace are laced with protections. No one is getting to her again without first having to go through *me*."

Maewen taps her mouth with a finger as she considers Tarrien's response. Whatever it was that I saw in her is now well-hidden once again.

"The whole thing sounds a lot bigger and more organized than I thought," she says. "Which is both a bad thing, and a good thing, I guess."

"How so? What is good about that fact?" I ask, genuinely curious.

"If it was simply a nutter—a necro or two gone

rogue—then potentially anything goes. The whole thing becomes completely unpredictable and could go off on any tangent, based on the whim of a literal madman. If there is someone in charge, and a group with an actual plan and a purpose, then we just need to work out what that purpose is, find those in charge, and thwart them. There is less chance of things going off-road on this, now that we know Rhiannon and Targon are controlling the whole thing."

"Off-road?"

"Just an expression. Never mind," she says. "So, Tarrien, you said they called it the Restoration Movement, when they were holding Indie?"

Tarrien nods.

"Hmm. I wonder if it is related to the Accord," Maewen says. "Restoring things to how they were before the Agreement was put in place. I've heard whispers over the years that there are such groups working covertly to that end. Nothing concrete, mind you."

Tarrien shrugs. "Possible. It wasn't long after the Accord Agreement was struck, between humans and supernatural creatures of all species, that these attacks first started. So, the timing fits."

"Why would that benefit my mother?" I ask. "Or your father, for that matter? Humans already know about supernaturals. Destroying the Accord now won't change that knowledge, though it might cause untold chaos if..."

I trail off as a sick feeling settles in my gut.

Chaos. Divide and conquer.

My mother always thrived on chaos. One of my earliest memories from when I was a young child, is sitting beside my parents at a Winter Solstice celebration. I remember the tiny smile on Mother's lips as she studied the happy revelries of our subjects in the fields and forests around us.

"Watch this, Rho, and remember the lesson." She reached out with her magic—silver strands that I could see even then were laced with darkness—and the happy crowd in front of us suddenly started to bicker amongst themselves. When actual physical fights broke out, I remember my father releasing a pained sigh and leaning over to frown at her.

"Leave them be, Rhiannon. It is Yule. Solstice is supposed to be a time of joy."

My mother pouted.

"Divide and conquer, Tryppton," she said. "You don't do enough of that, dear husband. Not nearly enough."

But she did relinquish her hold on the Winter Court revelers, and then leaned down to whisper in my ear. "When you are grown, I will teach you how to rule properly, Rho. Create chaos, cause division, and then whatever power you desire will be yours for the taking."

I blink hard as the memory stabs at my brain. If only I had known then what I know now...

I stare at Maewen who is frowning at me, no doubt because of what she perceives as my wandering attention.

"Chaos. That's what she wants," I say in a flat tone.

Beside me, Tarrien nods. He remembers my mother well enough, too.

"If the Accord is ripped away, there will be no rules in place to guide how we all live together," I say. "Peace and harmony will disappear, and chaos will reign. She wants to use that chaos to slide in and rebuild her power. I am certain of it."

"She sounds...well..." Maewen clears her throat and doesn't finish.

She sounds like a monster. Those are the words I know she held back. Those, or something similar. I don't blame Maewen for her almost-insult. My mother *is* a monster. She's the only fae I know personally, who has let the darkness that is in all magic to rise up and take control. I never knew, as a child, that those dark strands at her core are not meant to be visible at all.

There is darkness in all fae, but we must never give in to it. We cannot.

"The important thing is," Maewen says after a pause, "how do we find her and Targon, now?"

My turn to face her. "I have a few suggestions about that. We should—"

Maewen's phone rings loudly, cutting me off, and she releases a swear word I have never heard before.

"Not now." She rubs her eyes briefly before picking

up the device and answering the call in a gruff tone.

She really does seem overly tired. Does she not have anyone in her life to keep an eye on her and make sure she looks after her own health? Rests when she needs it?

"Another?" Maewen barks into the phone. "Where?"

She jumps up and moves away from us, over to the kitchen area. It is such a small space—and, of course, using my fae senses—I can still hear both sides of the conversation. Judging by the intent expression on Tarrien's face, he is listening in as keenly as me.

There has been another vicious attack, and it sounds like an abomination might have been involved.

"Three humans dead this time, boss," says a male voice on the other end of the line. "Do you want us to proceed in the usual way, or wait till you get here?"

"You know what to do, Durand. You might be new to *my* team but you've been with SUDAP long enough to know the drill. Cordon it off and get forensics in as soon as you can. The supe forensics team, not the standard. I'll be there shortly, but don't wait on my arrival."

"No problem."

She pokes at the phone screen, ending the call, and shoots us an apologetic look. "Sorry, Rhodri, Tarrien. We'll have to finish this tomorrow. Well, later today, I guess, given its now after two am. I need to be somewhere."

"An abomination attack. We heard," I say, and ignore her instant frown. "We will come with you."

"No," she says, speaking slowly as if Tarrien and I are children. "You will use your magic rings and head home to...well, wherever home is for you both, and leave this investigation to me. I suggest you return to my office at, say, midday, and we can take up our discussion then."

I open my mouth to dismiss her suggestion and scold her for her disrespectful attitude, but Tarrien gives a tiny shake of his head and touches his ring. I hear his voice then, in my mind. All winter warriors can communicate telepathically with the royal family, when it is required. The ring helps facilitate that communication.

Let her go, Rhodri. We can follow without her being aware of it. She's a stubborn one, he says. *As are all Renna's children.*

Yes, she is. This one...particularly so.

Maewen rushes around gathering a jacket and re-fastening the gun belt she had removed before we ate.

No point arguing, I tell Tarrien. We can work around her.

Clearly, Maewen is used to being in charge. So am I. Technically, given that banshees herald from the Winter Court, I am her monarch's heir, and that trumps her status as a police officer, no matter what realm she resides in.

She won't like it when we turn up unannounced, but perhaps she won't find out. And if she does?

A grin lifts my lips at the thought of that scenario. I can imagine those large hazel eyes flashing in annoyance as I announce that I can do what I wish. Whether Maewen likes it, or not.

I enjoy the idea of making her eyes shine bright with emotion—in annoyance...or in the throes of passion. Either would be pleasing to me.

She bends to fasten her boots and I can't help noticing the perfect roundness of her arse and the shapely length of her thighs in those skin-tight black trousers.

What would Maewen do if I stepped forward right this minute and pressed my burgeoning organ into her shapely rear, cradling my hard flesh in the soft valley of her folds? Clothing is nothing, to a fae. I could remove it all, in an instant. What would she do if I took her from behind, thrusting deep inside her channel and filling her with my manly need?

What would she sound like, if I were to run my hands up the long line of her back and around her ribs to cup the fullness of her breasts? Would she moan, if I squeezed her nipples tight? Or would her breath escape in a gentle mewl? Would her eyes remain hazel, or would they shift to a deep emerald green, telegraphing her need when I withdrew from her body and turned her so I could kiss her sexy mouth as deeply as I wish?

I accidently release a throaty growl at the thought of Maewen in the throes of passion. Maewen, kissing me, climbing into my arms and wrapping those sexy legs around my hips as I take her again, filling her with my hot and urgent seed.

She halts her frenetic movement and turns to stare at me, her gaze dipping briefly to the erection I cannot hide. Heat rushes into my cheeks as her mouth drops open. We remain there in a weird, frozen tableau. Tarrien clears his throat in an awkward fashion and grabs my arm. He opens a portal and drags me backward into the faerie path with him. Just before the light claims me, I note that Maewen's eyes have, indeed, become green.

It is only afterward, when we have travelled to the address we overheard during the phone call, that I realize Maewen did not volunteer any information during our discussion. She encouraged us to talk, and yet she shared little. A skill no doubt born of police training, and one that both annoys and intrigues me.

Inspector Maewen Jones is complex and fascinating, and when this disastrous situation with my mother is resolved, I intend to find out more about the banshee-hybrid police officer who refuses to supplicate herself to royalty.

I resolve to make it my mission to stare into her beautiful hazel-green eyes as she orgasms around my cock.

Chapter Three

MAEWEN

The investigation is orderly and well-underway when I arrive at the crime scene at a local warehouse. I have to tuck away that moment in my apartment, when I met Prince Rhodri's sensual gaze and read the intense sexual desire in his eyes. Now isn't the time to dwell on such things.

The shock of knowing a royal fae desires me—and a damn sexy royal fae, at that—reverberates right through my body, coalescing between my legs in an ache I haven't felt in far too long. God, as if I have time for a dalliance at the present time. Even one with someone who embodies my idea of the perfect male, at least in a physical sense.

I remind myself that he probably has sex all the time, and that such a look likely means nothing, coming from him. Fae are known for their casual approach to sexual relations, and I'm sure he was simply testing the waters to see if I would respond. I probably annoyed him, not genuflecting the way he expected, and he thinks he can control me with sex.

He certainly couldn't *really* want me. Not with that level of intensity.

I take a deep breath and huff it out slowly, trying to re-focus on the task at hand. Crime scene. Dead victims. People who can no longer speak for themselves and who need me and my team to help catch the violent perpetrators who did this awful thing to them.

My mind back on the job, I stride forward, pleased to see most of my team are already here. They are good at their work, and I trust them. Sergeant Durand has only recently joined my team from another divisional office, so I am not familiar with him personally but his positive reputation precedes him.

And apparently, he's dating my sister.

Well, one of my half-sisters, to be precise. My mother seems to have been quite prolific in the half-human, half-banshee child-making department, or so I understand. Up until recently, I had never met another human-banshee hybrid—even though I knew there were quite a few half-siblings out there. I was quite happy for things to stay that way.

I've never wanted the reminder of my banshee heritage. I like feeling human. I hate my fae side so much, I pay a fortune to keep my banshee magic contained.

I twirl the ring on my right pinkie finger as I do at every crime scene. It isn't superstition that causes me to clutch at the opal ring. I simply need the constant reassurance that the talisman remains in place and in working order.

Who would ever choose to be a banshee? Especially when my dream was to become a police officer and solve crimes, and in order to do so, I have had to steep myself in death at every turn.

The freedom from my banshee magic that the charm provides allows me to be human, and it allows me to pursue the dream I've had since I was ten years old and my two best friends at school—my *only* friends—were ripped to shreds outside the library by some kind of ravening monster that was never caught.

I was in the library at the time, taking a peek inside the thick copy of *Lord of the Rings* that the librarian said was way too advanced for my childish eyes. I wanted to prove her wrong, but I never got the chance.

One moment I was avidly reading a passage about evil riders, and the next, I was writhing on the floor, wailing and crying as horrifying waves of death and dying washed over me.

Two deaths. People I knew and loved. Innocent children, who were sitting on a bench outside doing nothing but chatting brightly with each other while they waited for their friend—*me*—to finish inside. Gone. Dead. And no one seemed to care enough to find out exactly what happened and why.

I realized later it wasn't apathy on behalf of the police, but a simple lack of knowledge about anything supernatural. SUDAP was still in its infancy back then, and when I told my dad I was going to join them one day and make sure no one else lost people they loved to the monsters, he begged me to steer clear of anything that might bring me into contact with more death.

"You love books," I remember him saying. "Why not train to be a librarian?"

"Death came *at the library*, Dad," I yelled back at him. "Nothing can stop it from coming, except maybe catching the bad guys so they can't do it again. I can't do that as a librarian."

He hasn't spoken to me for twelve years—not since the day I signed up as a recruit when I was eighteen.

I met the witch mage Topaz that same year, when I was investigating a break-in at her spell shop. That case turned out to be local teens expressing speciesism by targeting the businesses of those identified as supernatural. Witches are human, of course, but they are *more* than human, and as such often the target of narrow-minded bigots such as that teenage gang.

Topaz sold me the charm embedded in the opal. The talisman has proven a godsend since then, but she warned me there would likely be long-term consequences for denying my innate magic. She reminds me of the same every year when I return to boost the charm's power when it wanes. But no one else needs to know anything about those consequences. That is my own private hell to bear. It is the price of denying my fae-half, and it is one I am willing to pay. Over and over, if it means I can get on with the job and maybe stop even one monster from taking more innocent lives.

The hum of latent energy warms my fingers and I release my grip on the ring. The talisman does not yet need a top-up.

"Inspector." Luc Durand approaches me, his long lean form encased in a white forensic suit. With the pale vampire skin, his dark hair and blue eyes stand out against the suit more than usual. "Three dead. Human night workers, the manager tells us, who were rostered on to shift pallets ready for the trucks in the morning."

At my raised brow, he adds, "Electrical goods scheduled for local store delivery. Nothing untoward about the stock or the warehouse itself."

"And definitely not an attack by other humans?"

Durand shakes his head. "They were ripped apart, and partially eaten. I'd say, based on bite mark patterns, there were two attackers. Most likely both weres."

"Rogues working in unison again? Okay. Take some samples from the scene back to the office and run them through the calibration machine. If the same trace magic shows up, we can at least link it officially to the other attacks."

Durand nods as another team member, Jock, hands me a suit and gloves.

I kit up as I continue to talk to Durand. "It's likely the same perps piloting them, from the sound of it. Any sign of a medallion? Bracelet? Witnesses? Talk me through it."

We walk together toward the grim scene, and I silently send thanks to Topaz for her protection as I survey the carnage spread across the warehouse. A banshee cry denotes impending death, but even though these poor victims are clearly long gone, the miasma of death itself remains in the environment for some time. I feel the crawl of it over my skin, and I shiver.

Were it not for the mage's protective charm, I would be far more adversely affected than a touch of nausea and a case of the shivers, even though death has already been and gone.

I'm about to check in with the rest of my team regarding setting up a grid search when a flash of silver out of the corner of my eye catches my attention. The vampire beside me turns sharply. He jumps in front of me with a hiss.

His head twists side to side as he scans the environment, his incisors extended.

Slowly, I reach out and touch his shoulder. "All right, Luc. Calm down, now."

After a moment, he releases a sharp sigh, and his incisors retract. "Sorry, I'm still a bit jumpy after what happened to Aleah back in Hatton Grove. You're her sister, so...yeah. Just went into protect mode, then. Family, you know?"

His cheeks are faintly pink—the most embarrassment a vampire is ever likely to show—and amusement curves my lips upward. Amusement, coupled with surprised pleasure. The vampire sees me as *family*? Wow. He and Aleah must be really serious about one another.

Then I realize what the flash that caught our attention actually means, and my smile turns to a scowl. Sure enough, the two fae I thought had returned home to the Winter Court come strolling into my crime scene.

I growl deep in my throat, and Luc sends me a quick look.

"Not dangerous to us," he says. "That one on the left is Tarrien, Indigo's—"

"Yes. I know who he is."

"Do you know the other?"

"The Winter King's son. Prince Rhodri. I met him earlier tonight and he is annoying the crap out of me, already. I'll deal with them. You keep going here, and we'll all assemble for a briefing back at the office at nine am. I know you'll have gone to ground by then, but you can text me an update before the meeting."

Being a vamp, Durand tends to work mostly nights. It's a fallacy that vampires drop into unconsciousness the moment the sun rises, but they certainly do need to remain in a darkened room during the day time. Quite often, our vamp staff are set up under a work-from-home arrangement, so they can remain hidden in their lair, wherever that might be, and communicate via online arrangements.

So far, Durand seems to prefer action rather than computer work, which means, he's now my primary on-call night investigator.

"Done." Durand starts to leave, and then turns back, a light grin decorating his lips. "Go easy on them, boss. We need all the help we can get on this one."

He disappears quickly, before I can respond, and I wait for the recalcitrant faerie men to reach me.

"What the actual hell are you doing here?" I say. "I thought I told you—"

"You don't have the right to tell us what we can or cannot do." Rhodri cuts across me in a smooth voice, but his eyes shoot daggers. "I am royalty, and I will do as I wish."

Fine. I can shoot daggers right back, prince.

"I could still have you arrested for obstructing the course of an investigation, royalty or not. Ask your warrior about the special cuffs. He's had direct experience wearing those, haven't you, Tarrien?"

Rhodri turns to his companion, who looks uncomfortable.

"They are imbued with something that renders the wearer non-magic," Tarrien says. "I would not advise testing them out, sir."

Rhodri releases a short laugh. "Aside from the fact that you'd have to get the cuffs *on* us first"—he waggles his wrists as if taunting me—"surely, there's no real need for that, Maewen. We only wanted to see the scene and extend our assistance, should you need it. We are, after all, on the same side, here, are we not?"

I have no intention of arresting them, of course. But something about the prince seems to rub me the wrong way.

"Look, you both need to leave, so I can do my job. I am happy to meet you at noon—as we had already arranged."

I spread my arms to shepherd them away.

Tarrien backs away. The prince holds his ground a moment, before following suit. His sudden cooperation surprises me until Rhodri says, "We've already scouted around here as much as we need to. We have a sense of what happened. Definitely two abominations. Weres, if I'm not mistaken."

"You've already... *God*!" What I really want to say, is *fuck*. Or something even worse. I am proud of my own restraint.

Rhodri smiles sweetly at me. "Am I, by chance, annoying the *crap* out of you?" So, his fae ears obviously picked up my earlier conversation with Luc. "I apologize, Inspector Maewen Jones."

His tone confirms he doesn't mean it. Before I can respond, he turns to Tarrien.

"Let's head back to the palace. I need to speak with

Father and bring him up to speed on what's been going on. Gain his permission to mobilize some of the winter warriors."

"Really?" Tarrien asks, with a strange note in his voice that I don't understand. "Won't he—"

"He's still the king," Rhodri cuts in, his cheeks flushing. "I will obtain the permissions we need, and in the meantime, you rally those who are available and have them ready to go."

"Yes, sir."

They disappear in another flash of silver, leaving me with a hot mix of emotions churning in my belly.

I also have additional questions, now. Questions about what the hell might be going on behind the scenes at the Winter Court of Faerie.

RHODRI

The palace throne room is empty, as it often seems to be these days. When I was young, Father sat daily on the large throne up on the dais, Mother beside him. The palace was filled with a constant throng of courtiers and high-standing fae who gave life and vibrancy to the Court.

Winter Faerie was always full of life and laughter and high spirits. At least, so it seemed to my young and enthusiastic eyes.

Now, the rooms and halls are mostly silent. Icicles still hang from the ceilings, but their previous sparkle is gone. Now, the formations are merely ice, and not part of the magic of the Winter Court.

The fae are still around, but everyone moves in a more muted manner, without the joy or the energy of the past.

Mother's throne on the dais is long-gone, removed and burnt at the time of her banishment. Tryppton replaced it with another, mostly for my benefit in case I wished to sit beside him. Until recently, I have not been here long enough to use it.

Once I passed my teenage years, which occurs for fae around the age of one hundred and eighty, give or take, I spent years training with the winter army, learning to fight. That was followed by many more years travelling to other realms to see how different species live. I told myself I wanted to see how things are run outside of the Winter Court, but the truth is, I've been running from the responsibility I know is awaiting me here at home.

From what the head of the General Council tells me, Father spends most of his time these days moping around the palace hallways or wandering the snow-filled gardens, bemoaning times gone by and reminiscing about the past to whoever will listen.

He has some good days, when he graces the throne and receives visitors. At those times—when he seems more like his old self than ever—everyone's hearts fill with hope. But the good days are becoming less frequent and sometimes, like today, it feels as if the Winter Court is operating without anyone at the helm.

The General Council—a group of high-level fae nobility—have essentially taken over the day-to-day running of the Court, though technically, they still defer to King Tryppton for any decisions that need to be made. But the arrangement is merely a temporary measure, until the king recovers. Or until the heir apparent takes over.

I always knew that, one day, I would be expected to assume leadership of the Winter Fae, but that day seemed so far away. Fae are immortal, unless they are killed, of course, and to be a prince or princess of any fae court is usually to be someone whose role rarely progresses beyond that of heir apparent.

There has not been a change in king or queen within Faerie—in any Court—for as long as anyone can remember.

I have been quite content in the role of heir apparent.

Lately, though, I've begun to realize that it is not going to be enough. Someone has to take on responsibility for the Winter Court. The idea creates unwelcome pangs in my belly and my pulse rate increases every time I consider what that means.

Deposing my own father and taking control in his stead.

It sounds treasonous, even in my thoughts, but with a king who refuses to step up and rule, what other choice do I have? I am the only child of Tryppton and Rhiannon, and if I don't do what needs to be done, the Winter Fae will eventually be without a ruler at all.

To upset the balance in Faerie in any way is never wise, and the Winter Court in particular harbors a number of fae who are attracted more to the dark than the light.

It's just how it is; how it has always been. There is darkness in all of us, to some extent. Winter fae are more like humans in that regard, than perhaps our summer fae cousins.

While there is a strong and just leader on the Winter throne, the dark has no chance of rising up and taking over. Without such a leader, the balance is inevitably thrown out and chaos has a chance to rule.

My mother thrives on chaos, and the darkness within her has already taken over. What has happened to *her*, could happen to others, if the balance of power is allowed to teeter out of control.

It's not that Father is dying, or he is no longer a fair leader. Rather, his heart isn't in it, and hasn't been since the day he banished his wife, and that has weakened his rule over time.

There was a push recently, led by the Council, to find a new queen for Tryppton and try to drag him out of the doldrums into which he seems to have placed himself. Many fae with daughters of marriageable age became excited about the possibility that their child might become the next winter queen.

Word went around that a ball would be held, and the enthusiasm was unprecedented. But the idea fizzled out to nothing, when Father refused to cooperate.

"I'm still married to Rhiannon," he told the Council members when they called him to a meeting to discuss the idea of holding an event to choose a partner. "Why do I need a new queen?"

I remember the head of the Council, Lord Ruferne, looking over at me and subtly shaking his head. He approached me soon after that meeting, letting me know without saying it straight out that I need to start preparing to become the new leader of our people.

"Your father is weary, sir," Lord Ruferne said. "And the Winter Court needs strength, now more than ever. You are young, and perhaps lacking in experience, but you have both moral and physical strength. Our people need that."

I try to sit in with the Council at least two or three times a month so that, when the time comes, I will have some inkling of how our kingdom is actually run.

The conversation about becoming leader has replayed over and over in my mind ever since. How does one prepare to lead a whole realm of powerful and magical beings who embrace darkness as much as they do the light?

I love the Winter Court—its magics run deep in my veins. But I've never led anything or anyone in my life.

I don't know if I have the inner strength to become leader of the Winter fae, when the time comes.

I don't want the job.

But there's no one else suitable to take it on. One day—sooner rather than later—I am going to have to test out my inner fortitude and my leadership skills, and in doing so, force my father to step aside.

I pray I do not find whatever is inside me, wanting in the task.

I discover Father sitting on a bench seat in the palace garden, among a profusion of winter-flowering plants and shrubs. I understand why he enjoys it out here. The air is crisp and clear, and the perfume from many of the flowers such as winter jasmine and daphne, fills the air and creates an atmosphere of calm contentment.

I used to play out here when I was young, chasing my playmates—including Tarrien, come to think of it —around the bare tree trunks and along the snowy paths.

Summer fae often tease those from the Winter Court, wondering how we can bear to live in eternal cold. But there is such beauty here, such power in the majestic snow-filled landscape, that I cannot imagine ever wanting to be any other kind of fae.

"Father, how are you today?" I join him on the bench seat.

He looks older than I remember, and slightly hunched. *Gods, he looks like an old man, all of a sudden.*

Today is very clearly *not* a good day.

"I am well, son, very well. Though the winterberries are like droplets of blood against the snow, do you not think?"

"Um…" I follow the direction of his pointing finger. "Well, yes, I suppose the berries do look like blood. If you squint."

I take a deep breath and release it slowly. There's no point getting annoyed with him. He can't help it.

"I need to speak with you about something else today. Not the garden, Father. Something more important."

"Oh, of course." He drops his hand back to his lap, and he sits there, lethargic. He already seems fragile and frail. Will my news tip him over the edge into insanity? Should I remain quiet? Try to sort it out myself?

What would a true leader do?

Thoughts tumble through my brain. I am unsure of the right path, but in the end, I go with my gut instinct.

A true leader would lead. A true leader would make his own decisions, and start standing up on his own two feet instead of relying on his parent to make the decisions for him.

Time to grow up.

I decide to give him part of the truth, and test out his reaction. "There is a threat to the balance of power among the realms. A threat to the Accord Agreement that you signed, along with the other species. Do you remember that, Father?"

At his nod, I continue. "The threat is centered for now in the human realm, but if allowed to continue there, it may spill over and affect Faerie in a more direct manner. It may even affect our own Winter Court."

"That sounds bad, Rho."

Indeed.

"It is."

Sadness creeps over me as I see he is not going to ask anything about the nature of the threat. My father is much further along the road to decline than I realized. I pat the top of his hands still resting in his lap, trying hard to remember the proud and strong fae he once was.

"I am going to mobilize some of the winter warriors. I may need them to assist me in neutralizing the threat. I am going to make sure that the Winter Court remains safe. I promise you that, Father. I will do...what it takes."

I will go up against Mother, and I will stop her.

"Of course." Father nods again, and keeps nodding for longer than he should, as if his head is too heavy for his spindly neck to control. Eventually he stops. "You do what it takes. I know I can always rely on you for that."

"Of course, Father. Take care now. I will return soon."

I leave him in the garden, staring vacantly at the winterberries, and swallow down the bile that rises in my throat. How will Winter Faerie remain safe, moving forward, if our leader is no longer strong enough for the task?

Chapter Four

I find myself drawn back to Maewen's apartment in the hours leading up to dawn. I have the vague notion that someone should be keeping watch over her. Given it is my mother leading the enemy charge, I feel responsible for her safety.

I am tempted to port myself all the way into her apartment but I can hear tiny little snores, and I am certain she would not want to wake up and find me standing over her. I would not like to be placed in that situation myself, knowing someone had been watching me sleep without my permission. So, instead, I create myself a cushioned chair in the hallway outside her apartment door, take a seat, and create a protective bubble so I will not be visible to any early risers of the human variety.

She will likely still be angry when she wakes and

finds me here at all. My presence seems to annoy her greatly no matter what. But in all conscience, I cannot leave her alone. She might not act like a fae hybrid, but Maewen is still half-banshee, and as such, one of my Court's subjects. She, like her sisters—and indeed, like all the unfortunate human victims in this—could be a target of the Restoration Movement.

So far, it seems as if the abominations attack humans because they are easy to get to, and likely because they have little to offer in the way of defense. But obviously, Renna's children are potentially in danger from my mother, as well. Especially given Mother has now openly declared her desire to collect their banshee blood. Or their true names. Or both.

I wonder what Maewen's true name might be. I have three, being royal. Though I am aware she must have one, I cannot imagine her as anything *but* Maewen. It suits her. Unusual, tough and to the point, and yet somehow soft and vulnerable, all rolled up in that one, beautiful, word.

"*Maewen.*" Without meaning to, I whisper her name aloud.

My keen hearing picks up a stirring within the apartment, though it couldn't possibly be from my voice. I spoke too quietly to disturb her. Maewen releases a small moan, a sound that could denote either pain, or sexual arousal. *Damn it.* She seemed exhausted earlier. I should leave her be to sleep as long as she can, now.

I release a slow sigh, trying not to think of her long, curvy body tangled up in her bedsheets. I would make love to her in a heartbeat, should she wish it. She is one of the sexiest creatures I've ever laid eyes on and her pheromones call to mine in a way that is both frustrating, and tantalizing. But nothing will happen between us. Maewen has made it very clear that she is not interested in me in that way.

Pity. I sit straighter in the chair, trying to switch off my disobedient thoughts. I am determined to ensure no enemy will enter her premises on my watch. *Sleep, little banshee. Enjoy your rest. I will keep you safe. And I will try to stop thinking of you naked and begging for sex.*

As if she senses my thoughts and wants to be contrarily opposite, I hear sudden movement behind the door. The sound of someone thrashing about rises. Before I can wonder if she is in the throes of a passionate dream, Maewen's voice rings out in a sad and lonely wail. It is the most pitiful sound I've ever heard.

I'm torn as to what I should do. Should I leave her alone to ride out whatever nightmare clearly haunts her?

Another wail, only this one turns into a full-throated scream. I can't help myself. I port to the inside of the apartment and rush to her side.

She is still sleeping, even as she screams and sobs and thrashes around. I lift her up and onto my lap, pushing aside the bedcover that is, indeed, as tangled as I imagined. Though not for the same positive reasons I envisioned while outside her door. She is wearing an old gray tee-shirt through which her erect nipples are clearly visible. The length of the top is such that it only barely covers her lower body. I try to ignore the parts the tee-shirt doesn't cover, and concentrate on cradling her tense body in my arms. I rock her gently back and forth. Tears pour from her still-closed eyes as her scream fades into a series of heart-wrenching sobs.

"Shh, it's all right, I've got you. Shh, calm down, little banshee, calm." I begin to croon in my own language, not even sure what I'm saying, until the tension leaves her body and she collapses like a rag doll fully against my chest.

"What... *Rhodri*? What on earth? Ohhh..." She shudders and her sobs begin anew, only this time her eyes are half open and she clutches at my shirt with both fists. "I can't bear the agony of it. Hold me, Rhodri. *Please*."

"I am, dear one. It is all right, I've got you."

"Oh, God. Make me forget."

Make her forget... *what*? And how? I don't understand what is going on in her mind. It is obvious she is hurting, though I cannot tell whether the pain is physical or mental. Perhaps it is both?

She suddenly opens her eyes fully and gazes up directly into my face. The color of her irises is no longer hazel, but pure emerald. I could drown in those glorious green depths. My mind goes blank, and I will it to stay that way. Now is not the time to be thinking lascivious thoughts. Now is not the time to be noticing that she has no underwear on beneath the too-short tee-shirt and that her arse—her bare arse—fits perfectly in my lap.

I pat her awkwardly on the back and attempt to remove my arms from around her. I slide her off my lap and back onto the bed, trying to use mind power to force my burgeoning hard-on to shrivel up and disappear. It ignores me, growing by the second as Maewen places a hand each side of my face and drags me down to her.

"Kiss me," she whispers against my lips.

I can't believe I'm trying to dissuade her, but this feels wrong, as if I'm taking advantage of her in a moment of vulnerability. "I don't think...Maewen, not now. We should wait until..."

Too late. Her lips capture mine with a ferocity I cannot resist. Her tongue slips into my mouth and without thought I accept and begin to kiss her back. The kiss is divine, instantly igniting further heat in my groin and putting paid to any chance I have to control my growing need.

When she moans, her breath flutters into me, the sound unlike her earlier panicked cries. This sound is clearly seated in desire rather than distress. I sink my hands into her long, tangled hair and cradle her head, feasting greedily on her proffered mouth and allowing her to feast on me in return.

We finally break apart, both of us panting. Somehow, we have ended up kneeling on the bed facing each other. I am not sure when my hands dropped from her head down to her butt cheeks. Her *bare* and deliciously curvy butt cheeks.

Heat flares in my face, but even as I begin a stumbling apology, my hands remain on her arse as if they are separated from my brain and therefore non-cooperative. "I apologize, Maewen. I do not wish to take advantage of you in such a—"

"I *want* you to, Rhodri." Her voice is fierce, thrumming with desire that she is making no effort to hide. "I want to be taken advantage of, right now. By you. It's just sex, isn't it? Nothing more. Don't you want to? It will help me...forget..."

She shoves at my chest, encouraging me to lie back. *Just sex.* I know that phrase well. I've used it myself, regularly. Up until this moment, sex has always been nothing more than physical gratification, in the many encounters I've had in my life. And I expect it will be the same, with Maewen. Why would it be anything...more?

My heart pounds as she shucks her tee-shirt over her head and throws it to the side. My stomach swirls, as if an army of butterflies have taken up residence in my belly.

If it is just sex, then why are my hands shaking as I take a moment to remove my own clothing before laying back on her soft downy bedcover as she directs? Why not simply morph the clothing off quickly, as I would normally do, and get to the act of intercourse without second-guessing every thought, every action, every emotion? Without anticipating what it might feel like when she slides her hungry body down onto my waiting erection...

Why do I continue to wonder if this is what she really wants, or if it is the right thing to do at this time, when minutes earlier she was so clearly in a distressed state?

Rational thought drifts away as she straddles me and stares down at my cock with hunger in her gaze. It is pointing skyward and clearly transmitting how much I want her. I can't hide the fact that my desire feeds on hers.

She reaches out and fists my flesh, up and down, several times. The opal and silver ring she wears on her smallest finger flashes as she moves. The sight is mesmerizing, the sensation exquisite, and I shiver beneath her touch, afraid I won't be able to last as long as she wishes.

Desire is so strong in the air I can almost smell its heady essence. A growl releases from my constricted throat.

"By all the winter gods, Maewen, I feel this is not good timing, but I...oh yes. That is so damn good." My voice strangles, and I swallow hard. "I want you badly, little banshee-human."

She removes her hand, tracing a circle around the tip of my organ before she does so.

"I'm sorry," she says, in a strange tone. "You're not taking advantage of me at all, Rhodri. It's the other way around. But there isn't time to explain. There isn't time for anything other than...oh, my God!" She descends, her body sinking onto my hard flesh until I am seated deep within her channel. "Yes!"

She begins to ride me, with a desperation that lends urgency to her movements, and all doubt, all thought, disappears from my mind. I lose myself in the heat and the slick wet tightness of her body around me. The clenching of her inner muscles as her movement intensifies draws a shocked gasp from my lips.

A wild abandon seems to take her over at the sound. She moves frantically, her breasts wobbling and her breath coming in uncontrolled pants. I grab her around the hips, trying to hold her steady as I thrust up and into her, meeting her grinding movements with my own. The slap of flesh on flesh, and the grunts and groans and moans from both of us fill the air, until I cannot hold on a moment longer.

"Mae, I can't hold on. I'm going to—"

"Yes, Rho! Come! Come hard. Come now!"

I roar as I do her bidding, releasing my hot seed deep inside her as she gasps and shudders and tips over the edge a second behind me. She falls into her own climax with a stifled scream, her inner muscles clenching violently around my flesh and her fingernails digging deep into my upper arms as she collapses forward onto my chest.

MAEWEN

Oh, my God. That was incredible. And insanely stupid.

I can't believe how good that felt. I can't believe I just did that. With Rhodri.

When I woke from my nightmare, he was just *there.* I didn't even think about it. I just grabbed him, hoping at most for a moment's escape from the agony of my nightmares. Instead, I got so much more.

I owe Rhodri an explanation, at the very least, and I will provide it. In a moment. For now, I don't want to move. I can still feel his flesh seated deep inside me, his heart rate fast beneath my cheek where I lay sprawled on his muscled chest. His skin against mine is soft and warm, yet the firmness of muscle beneath the silken layer is equally as enticing.

A soft outer layer, encasing hard steel.

A perfect combination in a lover.

He wraps his arms around me, stroking my back, and I see the crescent marks on his biceps.

"Oh, God, I'm so sorry. I drew blood."

I lift a hand and run my fingers over the marks left by my fingernails. When did I even do that? Heat rushes into my face and I turn briefly into his chest, hiding from him. Hiding from everything.

I feel his lips on my hair as he places a gentle kiss atop my head.

"It is nothing," he says. "Doesn't hurt at all. I am glad you enjoyed yourself enough to mark me."

I unfurl from my position and slide off him to lie by his side.

He shifts a little beside me. "You said it was just sex. But that did not feel like *just sex*," he says. There's a question in his statement, one that he hasn't voiced, but I know I have to address it.

I release a slow sigh. "No. It didn't feel like that to me, either. But I can't let it be any more than that."

He props himself up on one elbow and stares down at me, a quizzical line forming between his brows.

"Why not?" he asks. "What was it, then, to you?"

I reach up to smooth away his frown line. "It was... oh, how to explain it?"

I sit up and hug my knees into my chest. I'm not prudish enough to worry about whether or not I'm covered at this point in time, but the protective gesture makes me feel slightly more contained and in control.

As if hunching in over my own knees is likely to change anything.

"Several years ago, I bought a charm off a mage." I point briefly to my opal ring.

He takes my hand and studies the ring, before gently releasing me. There's a knowing look in his eyes. "I wondered how you were getting by as a banshee dealing with death."

I laugh, the sound short and lacking in humor. "I suppose you could say I'm getting by. The charm certainly helps keep the banshee magic tamped down to almost non-existent while I'm awake, but there's a cost. A consequence."

"Of course, there is," Rhodri says in a gentle tone. "If you deny what is natural, then nature will find a way of re-balancing itself. It is the way of things. If you force your fae magic into a box, it will find a way to bounce back out, sometimes even stronger than it was before."

"Yes, that's exactly what happens. It's as if everything that is held back while I'm awake has to be released somehow, sometime... So, when I sleep, when I dream...well, they're nightmares, really. Constant, terrifying nightmares..."

So much horror is unleashed in my dreams that I cannot bear it. And yet, I have no choice. Not if I want to keep being a cop. I have to keep using the charm.

"I don't sleep much," I admit.

When I slant a glance up at him, his brows have risen and I can almost see the question right there on the tip of his tongue. I move my hand in a gesture designed to stop him before he asks why I do it.

"I can't do my job—I can't be *human*—if I'm curling up in a ball every time someone nearby starts to die."

His non-committal grunt speaks volumes, as does his judgmental gaze.

"I hate my fae heritage, Rhodri. *Hate* it!"

He finally sits up too, only he turns his back to me and slides his legs off the bed before standing up. I study his rigid shoulders as he gathers his clothing and dresses quickly, and I realize he must have taken offence.

"I don't hate all fae," I clarify. "I don't hate *any* fae. Just my own banshee half."

"Not my problem," he answers coolly, still not looking at me. "But I have obviously overstayed my welcome."

"You don't understand!"

Now he does turn and look, and his eyes are a glacial blue, not warm like they were minutes earlier. "No. I do not understand. I am the future king of the Winter Court of Faerie. I love our realm, our people, our magics, with all my heart. Do you think all fae are good? Kind? Do you think all Winter Court magic is sparkles and snowmen? Of course, it isn't. There is dark magic as well as light. Good as well as bad. And yet, all of it goes to make up who we are. Every Winter Court fae is connected, through our magics. Even you, Maewen.

"How can you hate something that you *are*? How

can you hate something so wonderful and powerful, as your own magic? Your *gift!*"

"Gift? You call sensing death—*living* death—every time it happens around you, a gift? I don't have any magic, other than that. And it didn't help my friends, when they died. Children. Torn apart. I couldn't do a damn thing about their deaths, except wail and cry and live it right along with them. I don't call that a gift. I call it a fucking curse!"

I don't realize tears are streaming down my cheeks until one of them plops off the edge of my jaw and drops to the bedcover in front of me.

I scrub at my eyes, embarrassed. Rhodri's previously fierce expression softens a touch, but he doesn't approach me. Clearly, I have crossed a line of some kind, in his estimation.

"I am sorry you feel that way, Inspector Maewen Jones. But I am glad—even though you wish to deny your fae half—that you have your police work to sustain you. May it last many years, and bring you much joy."

A flash of silver, and he's gone. I can't even blame him for the sarcastic tone. I get why he's offended. But I can't change who and what I am. And I can't change how I feel.

I'm a police officer, first and foremost, and I have to focus on that. It's the only way I can ever hope to get any kind of justice for my friends. It's the only way any of the victims out there will ever have the opportunity for justice. If I can't do my job, I will fail those who have no voice left to speak up for themselves.

If I allow my banshee power free reign, then I might never be able to find and stop the abominations, or those who control them.

Chapter Five

More sleep is out of the question for what little remains of the night, so I end up back at the office earlier than planned, with a strong coffee in one hand and a donut in the other. It might be a cliché breakfast for a cop, but hot, sugar-coated and jam-filled donuts are a treat I only allow myself once in a while.

Today, I need a treat, and I have to suppress a delighted moan as I bite into the dough through the sugary crust, and strawberry jam oozes into my mouth.

The supe technicians—known within the division as the techies—are already at work, testing some new evidence that came in from the crime scene last night. I watch them for a while, finishing my breakfast and listening to their friendly back and forth banter. It seems as if nothing ground-breaking has been uncovered in the lab at this point, so I wander back to my corner office and prepare for the team briefing.

Luc Durand texts me just before nine. *Morning boss, confirming another medallion found at the scene last night. Clutched in the hand of one of the vics. Purple trace, so techies should calibrate it this morning. Have a good day.*

The briefing proceeds smoothly, and I stare around the room at my team, pride filling me at the eclectic mix of species who all work so well together. About half are human, and the rest are made up of shifters—a couple of weres, a panther, and a bear—plus a handful of witches and wizards. Two fae from the Summer Court are slated to join our team soon, but they will be the first of any fae to join us, other than me. The three vamps on the team are likely tucked up in bed somewhere.

The team make-up could be a disaster waiting to happen, but it isn't. We are all dedicated to our common cause of ensuring justice for victims of crime, no matter who they are, and I stare around at the sea of faces, knowing I can rely on each and every one of them. I start the briefing with a word of thanks for their loyalty and enthusiasm, before going around the room to hear from each member so we can pool our knowledge and plan next steps.

Nothing new arises, until one of the techies—a human named Jeb—pops his head into the briefing room just before we finish.

"Got it!" His voice is excited. "It's a match with the

trace on that bracelet the dead necro was holding. The one brought in last week."

Even though I hoped for something like this, the news is unexpected. I jump to my feet, my heart speeding up, as a hum of excitement ripples through the room. "Fantastic, Jeb! So, now that it's matched—"

"Now that we've matched it exactly, we'll have a much better chance of figuring out how one device controls the other, and once we do that, we might be able to create an app that senses the same pattern of activity around the city. Even, before it happens, not just at the time of a piloted attack."

"An app?"

"Well, a charm, I guess. But we can place it into an app that the teams can load up onto their phones." He grins. "Trust me, boss."

"I do trust you, Jeb. I trust everyone here in the room." I think about what he's said for a moment. "So, we might not be able to stop the attacks altogether— yet—but this will give us a chance to sense them when they're just gearing up to happen? If we can get there quickly...oh, this is fantastic news. Well done."

"Thank you, boss. Can I...?" He gestures, and I nod.

"Of course. Get back to it, and let me know the second you come up with anything more."

He disappears back out the door, and I let the buzz of hopeful chatter continue for a minute or two before I dismiss the team. They all need something positive to focus on. We've been on this case so long without a breakthrough. This development—while minor at the moment—is still a significant step forward, and if we can start to predict where attacks might take place...

I head back to my office with a large grin decorating my face. A grin that falters and disappears when I see the two tall fae waiting outside my door. *Damn!*

"I forgot I was meeting the two of you. Okay, come on in."

Tarrien has a serious expression on his face. Rhodri appears aloof. I try not to meet the prince's eyes as I sweep past, though his fresh scent rises in my nostrils and I can feel the heat emanating from his body. My system kicks into overdrive, as does my imagination, which I try to tamp down.

I do not want to remember what His Royal Highness looks like when he's just about to orgasm.

I do not want my traitorous woman bits to start aching every time he enters the room.

Heat warms my cheeks and I take my time shuffling around behind the desk, before finally gesturing them to sit.

Tarrien accepts my invitation. Rhodri remains standing, his hands tucked behind his back and a thin-lipped expression causing his already prominent cheekbones to seem even more defined than before.

Man, he is so handsome, despite the icy look in his eyes as he studies a spot somewhere above my head. I guess physical beauty is an advantage that comes with being a royal fae.

"Okay then, what've you got?" I direct my question to Tarrien, who opens his mouth to answer. But he is beaten to it by Rhodri.

"You first, this time," the prince says. "What do *you* have, Inspector?"

I try hard not to grind my teeth, and instead attempt a smile. Both men blink and recoil slightly, so I'm not sure I succeed in imparting pleasantness. I consider what to share, and decide there's no harm in letting them know what we've just discovered.

"Right, well, we've managed to identify a pairing in a bracelet and a medallion, both found with purple trace magic at violent crime scenes. This is good news —may even lead to being able to predict where an attack might happen next."

Tarrien's face lights up, and even Rhodri relaxes noticeably. Finally, he steps forward and takes the empty chair in front of my desk.

"That is good news," he says, in a tone noticeably warmer than before. "Tarrien, share your news with the Inspector, if you will."

The Inspector? So, clearly, we are not back on first name terms just yet. But then Tarrien speaks and I forget my issues with Rhodri.

"My father contacted me," Tarrien says. "It's the first time since his exile many years ago that anyone in our family has heard from him."

"What?" My eyebrows shoot up, and I lean forward, my mind racing. "How did he contact you?"

"He projected, through a mirror. I think he might have been trying for a while to get a hold of me, but I've been staying with Indigo in her apartment, and it is fully protected. It was only when I was waiting for her to finish a performance that I happened to be in her theater dressing room."

I gasp. "Oh, we need to—"

"All sorted," Tarrien cuts across me. "I now have better protections in place over the theater, too."

I nod, thankful. I may be reluctant to engage with my banshee siblings or fully embrace my fae heritage, but they are still family, and as such, I could not bear to see either of them harmed.

"He spoke to you through Indie's dressing room mirror? What did he say? What does he want?"

"Information," Tarrien says flatly.

Rhodri clears his throat and I turn my attention his way. He seems to have forgotten his annoyance toward me, at least for the moment. His eyes are bright with enthusiasm as he says, "I think we can use this to our advantage."

This time my smile is genuine. "Exactly what I was thinking."

Rhodri blinks, and we stare at each other for a long moment as if unsure how we should behave with each other. Indeed, I don't know how to catalogue the emotions he raises within me. One moment I want to punch his supercilious nose, and the next, I can't imagine anything I want more than his wickedly sexy lips feasting on my most intimate of places.

Butterflies rise in my belly and I clench my fists together on the desk top, determined not to release a betraying moan or groan.

After an uncomfortable pause, in which Rhodri's eyes rest on my clenched fists and change from clear blue to a deep cerulean, Tarrien coughs. The sound interrupts whatever is between the prince and me.

"Father seemed very interested in what was uncovered in the Badlands," Tarrien says. "He wanted to know whether there are any significant investigations into the abominations. On top of that, he started sounding me out about what sort of protections might be in place for Indigo and Aleah, if any. It was all very casual and innocent-sounding, couched between queries about how Mother and the rest of the family is faring, but it is far from innocent."

"Indeed." I lean back in my chair and study the ceiling, thinking hard. If we can somehow lure Targon out... "It sounds as if he's still interested in capturing a banshee for himself, or for his so-called queen. What if you use me as bait?"

"That could work," Tarrien says.

At the same moment, Rhodri says, "Absolutely not!"

I bring my gaze down to the prince and stare hard at him. "Why not?"

"Yes, why not, Rhodri? If Father and Rhiannon are after banshee blood, for whatever reason, then using Maewen to find them is an excellent idea." He falters at Rhodri's glare. "Isn't it?"

"It is far too dangerous for Maewen." Rhodri's tone is full of indignation.

"She's a cop. She's trained—"

"Look at what almost happened to Indigo. You should know better than to risk Indie's sister to potentially the same fate, Tarrien. You know the power my mother and your father wield. How dark it is. Shame on you."

"I'm merely agreeing with Maewen. I don't think—"

"Maewen is still a ban—"

"Guys, please." I hold up a hand. "Put them away. Tarrien is right. I am a police officer and I have been trained for dangerous situations. Not only that, but I have a whole team—hell, a whole department— behind me on this."

"Put what away?" Rhodri asks.

I roll my eyes and point at his groin. Tarrien snickers. Rhodri looks down at himself, and when he lifts his head, his cheeks are a satisfying pink.

My lips quirk. I didn't expect to enjoy teasing him so much. Clearly, he has not spent as much time as his warrior friend here in the human realm, at least, not to the level where he can fully understand all the nuances of human behavior. I have to admit it is rather fun making a royal fae prince blush.

He scowls and shifts in the chair.

I take the opportunity to add, "It isn't up to either of you to say whether I do this or not. It's up to me. And I say, yes. It's actually a good idea, if I do say so myself. We know they're behind this, but we don't know where they are located, at present. If we can lure them out...*yes*. Let's do it."

Rhodri's gaze turns frosty. "But—"

"No buts. Can you contact him again, Tarrien?"

"I believe so. He provided an incantation that I can use if and when I'm ready to reach out to him. He said if I use the incantation, he'll know it and be in touch."

"Good." My mind races, trying to figure out what we might need to set this up. "Can you let slip that you're also guarding another of Indigo's sisters? As in, me? Maybe let him know you're having a hard time of it due to my job in SUDAP. Nothing more than that at this stage, otherwise he'll know he's being played."

Tarrien nods, as Rhodri says, "I still think this is a bad idea. A very bad idea. Your father might be driven by his infatuation with my mother, Tarrien, but Rhiannon..." He shakes his head. "My mother has a darkness in her that terrifies even me. I saw it many times, when I was young, but I didn't fully understand the extent of it until recently. She is evil, and I do not want to put you in evil's way, Maewen. Please reconsider."

Why is Rhodri so invested in my welfare? By his stiff manner, I am certain he is not used to pleading his case. I guess, as a fae prince, he usually just states what he wants and others make it happen. The knowledge that he seems to have my wellbeing at heart softens my response.

"Don't you think it's time we stop this carnage, Rho?"

I don't mean to use the shortened version of his name. It just slips out naturally, and I only realize I've done it when Tarrien's brows rise and he shoots a curious look between the prince and me.

Rhodri ignores his warrior, keeping his gaze steady on me. I try a small smile, and see the beginnings of wry acceptance in his eyes.

"It has been going on far too long," I add. "At this moment I can't think of another way to draw them out. Can you?"

Silence fills my office, and Rhodri's lips tighten. But he doesn't say any more about vetoing the plan, and eventually I nod.

"Right. So, Tarrien, you contact your dad and set things in motion, and I'll brief the team here at my end to be ready to go. Let me know as soon as you hear back."

I stand up, assuming they'll immediately head off back to Faerie. Tarrien touches his ring and silver light from the resultant portal materializes in the office.

Rhodri jerks his head. "You go. I'll meet you back at

the palace, Tarrien. My quarters."

Tarrien nods and disappears. Rhodri folds his arms and stares at me.

"I don't want anything to happen to you, Mae. I was angry with you, earlier, for wanting to deny your fae heritage. I still don't understand that. But I..." He pauses and a frown appears fleetingly on his face. "I find myself liking you, more than I want to. More than I ever expected to. And the thought of someone —*especially* my own mother—draining your lifeblood, is one I cannot tolerate. I do not wish any harm to come to you. Not if I can help it. But I don't really know how to protect you. You seem far too independent to *need* protection, even when I want to provide it."

My cheeks warm at his words. He likes me? More than he wants to? I should be offended at that, but I'm not, because I know exactly what he means.

"I like you too, Rho." I lift my lips in a brief grin. "Far more than I expected to. But I'm a grown woman, and like I said earlier, I'm very good at taking care of myself."

Rhodri doesn't reply.

I shrug. "Always have been. I love that you want to protect me—no one has really ever offered that before and it makes me feel valued—but I truly don't need it. I'm *happy* to be bait, and lure them out, if it means another step toward ending this nightmare. I have no intention of letting things get far enough to actually risk life. Either mine, or anyone else's."

Acting on instinct, I step around the desk toward him, reaching out to rest a hand on his folded forearms. The muscles ripple beneath my fingers, as if in response to my touch. It is almost as if electricity passes between us every time we're near one another. Is that because he's royal? Or fae? Or is it simply pheromones?

I've had lovers before—very occasional ones, due to my focus on career—but I've never felt this sense of physical connection with anyone.

My belly clenches as his scent rises around me. What *is* that scent? It isn't like anything I've ever experienced on a mortal guy. It invades my system until all I can think about is pressing up against him. Losing myself in his embrace. My body shifts almost of its own accord and I lean into him. He unfolds his arms and holds my upper arms, his hands caressing gently up and down. Tendrils of desire squirrel through me.

I clear my throat, trying to bring things back to the matter at hand. "I'll be fine. And we'll get them, soon. I feel it in my bones."

He cups my chin, looking deep into my eyes, and warmth spirals out from his touch. "In your bones? That's your fae power, speaking to you, Mae. Let it free, and you might find it helps rather than hinders you in the future."

He bends his head, until his lips just graze my hair.

"I will allow you to do this, if you agree to let me be part of the team backing you up."

Allow? A laugh bubbles up and out before I can stop it. *Yeah, no, mate.*

I open my mouth to speak and he tilts up my face. *God, that wicked grin of his is so sexy.* My denial withers away to nothing.

"This is not negotiable," he says. "I know my mother better than most. I can be of immense value in this operation. I feel it. In my bones."

Before I can become annoyed about having my own words thrown back at me, he leans in and captures my lips in a brief, gentle kiss. Thoughts fly away as my whole body lights up with need. I think his hand brushes the back of my neck, causing a shiver to run down my spine. Or is that from the kiss, feather-light and yet, so full of promise?

Then he breaks off the kiss, stepping back and away. I feel a strange sense of loss.

He shoots me a crooked grin. "See you again soon, Inspector Maewen Jones."

He disappears in a spectacular blaze of silver light, leaving me torn between laughter, annoyance, and simmering desire as the imprint of his lips on mine remain long after he has vanished.

I consider the plan we've decided upon, trying to work out solutions to all possible scenarios.

Bait. With the royal heir to Winter Faerie's throne trailing after me. What could possibly go wrong?

Chapter Six

RHODRI

I don't want Maewen to be bait for my mother. I cannot bear the thought of Rhiannon's dark evil sucking the life out of Mae and draining her dry. And yet, if the plan goes wrong, that is exactly what might happen. I know the plan makes sense, but it is hard to trust in it completely, when the stakes are so high if we lose.

That is assuming, of course, that Tarrien will be able to contact his father and convince him that he is, in fact, struggling to protect at least one additional banshee.

I meant what I said to Maewen about being part of her team. If we do manage to lure out Targon or my mother, there are any number of things that could go wrong. If either of them somehow slip through SUDAP's clutches, I have as much chance as anyone of distracting them and holding their attention while others swoop in to secure them.

In the meantime, all I can do is return to Faerie and speak to my father about raising the full winter army. In theory, I will ask his permission, but the reality is more complicated than that, given his poor health. Regardless, I will ready the army for war, just in case.

The plan is rather frustratingly nebulous and up in the air at present, and dependent on Tarrien to initiate the contact—which is why I planted the small tracking device and microphone in the collar of Maewen's shirt. She may or may not still have that shirt on, when everything kicks off, but it was the only thing I could think of in the short time we spent in her office. At the very least, I can keep track of her over the next several hours. In that time, I can figure out something more long-term to try and keep her safe.

I cannot stop thinking about the sexy detective with her long, curvy body and the way she looked when she was mounted and riding my need.

The way her back arched so flexibly as she sank deep into her own arousal. The way her mouth dropped half-open and her eyes drifted closed as her channel muscles tightened and clenched around me. The delicate mewling sound that erupted from her throat at the moment of her climax.

My organ hardens every time I am near her. My mind fills with thoughts of what it might be like if we both choose consciously to make love with each other, enjoying the desire and the building need without the specter of her nightmares—or her need to forget—hanging over us.

Sex with Maewen was fleeting and she clearly used me to assuage her inner demons. It should have been passably enjoyable, nothing more, given the reason behind it. And yet, the experience was so much more than I expected. I believe it may have been the same for her.

What would it be like, if I chose to seduce Mae the way I think she should be seduced? In a manner that is slow and decadent and filled with every pleasure I can imagine? Will she allow herself to fully enjoy it, instead of remaining tense and filled with unspoken worry? Will she truly be able to let go and simply enjoy whatever this is, between us?

I can't stop my imagination from heading down dangerous and unchartered paths, whenever it comes to Maewen. Not even now, when I am back home in the winter palace and awaiting an audience with the king. When I arrived, I was informed that this is a rare good day, when Tryppton is actually in possession of most of his faculties and is receiving visitors in the throne room.

I shift uncomfortably, trying to tamp down thoughts of Maewen. It is not seemly, for the Winter Prince, to walk into the throne room while daydreaming about a girl. Especially not if the king is back to his old self. I need to concentrate.

When I am finally granted an audience, the courtiers already in the room part to allow me passage. I approach the throne and bend a knee, bowing my head. Even the heir apparent must adhere to protocol.

"Father." I remain kneeling until the king indicates I may rise.

"Son. What further news have you, from the mortal realm? What news...um...err..." He clears his throat, his expression eager and somehow sad. We both know he's asking about Mother.

We both know he doesn't want to hear the truth.

I shake my head slightly and the king visibly relaxes, slumping back a little on the throne.

His demeanor is vastly improved from the last time I left him, staring vacantly at the winterberries and imagining them as droplets of blood. But I can see the effort it is taking to hold himself upright on the throne, and the faint tremor in his hands clutching the chair arms. The threat of his mind retreating to somewhere else hovers on the edge of my awareness.

Father is not okay, even if he gives the opposite impression to most of the courtiers in this room.

"There has been an escalation in the attacks on humans, Father. I am working with the human police division, SUDAP, to follow a number of leads."

"You? A prince of the Winter fae, working with humans? Is that seemly, Rhodri? You are heir to the throne. *This* throne." Tryppton smashes one of his hands down on the arm of the chair, before patting it as if he didn't mean to be so forceful. He gives a small, embarrassed-sounding cough. "You need to ensure you behave in a manner suitable to your stature, son."

"Of course, Sire." I lower my gaze briefly, so he can't read the accusation in my expression. If it wasn't for his lack of action in relation to Rhiannon and Targon, there would likely be a whole lot of beings still alive today. I grind my teeth together, until I manage to rein in my temper.

"Last time we spoke, you requested permission to mobilize some of the winter warriors."

If he remembers that conversation, then he knows I didn't request permission. He also knows I won't embarrass him with a denial in front of everyone here.

I raise my head and narrow my eyes at him. "I remember. I have already done so, in readiness. *Sire.*"

The air cools around me as a sub-zero frost descends. Everyone in the throne room stills, as if they can sense the tension between father and son.

"In readiness for *what*?" My father's voice drips with ice, a reminder that he may be physically and mentally absent most of the time, but he is still King of the Winter Court of Faerie.

Well, I am the prince of that same court. I am the heir, as he just pointed out. I stare hard at him. Humans may think I am old at four hundred and thirty-five years, but in fae terms that is still relatively young. Right now, I feel like a human sixteen-year-old standing up to my parent for the first time, and I do not like that feeling at all. I might be young, but I am not *that* young.

I have had enough.

"In readiness to stop the deaths, Father. To end this decades-long issue that is taking life after innocent life. Don't you care? Don't you want to end this, as I do? You were the one who signed the Accord, on behalf of our people. You were the one who agreed that we should all live in harmony, no matter what species or realm we hail from. No matter where we live, whether we hold magic in our veins or not. *You* were the one who taught me, when I was young, that we should hold no hatred in our hearts for those different to ourselves. What happened to that sentiment, Father? What happened? Your detachment is the equivalent of condoning such behavior. Just because *she*—"

"Enough!" My father's roar reverberates through the room so loudly that some of the ever-present icicles drop from the ceiling to spear the floor. Luckily, no one is injured by the falling debris. Guards rush in to the room, swords and spears at the ready, until Father waves them away with a suddenly weary hand.

"Don't mention her again in this realm. *Ever*."

I incline my head, hearing the tremble in his voice. Pain for what was, and for what might have been, grows in my heart. He is done. I see it. They *all* see it.

"All right, Father. Not while you remain on the throne."

He rises, and instantly, he transforms into the old

and careworn man I saw on my previous visit in the palace garden. Gray strands pepper his dark hair, and his movements are slow and arduous as he steps down from the dais and shuffles across the floor to stand in front of me. He was always taller than me, by at least a head, but now, I realize I have to look down to meet his gaze.

My immortal royal father—my *king*—is an old and doddery man. Standing beside him like this, seems to highlight that fact to everyone standing around watching, and it seems wrong. Disrespectful. I hunch a little, trying to become smaller.

He smiles at me, a sad, tremulous parody of a smile, and pats me on the arm.

"You don't need my permission, anymore. We both know that." He slants a glance around the room. "They all know it, too. You said you would do what you had to do."

So, he remembers that part of our previous conversation, as well.

"I did. And I will."

His eyes close briefly.

"I know, son. You have the strength for it. More than I ever had. More than I ever will. I bid you farewell, Rho. And take care. The darkness in *her* was only a speck, in the beginning, just as it is in all of us. But in her, it grew. It grew so big, there was no room for the light. I don't believe there is anything of *her* left now, at all."

He gently squeezes my arm, and then shuffles past me. I turn and watch his departure, my heart hurting for so many reasons, and I do not move from my spot until well after everyone else has left the room.

MAEWEN

Midnight, and once again I'm only just leaving the office. I will have to break this habit, one day. I will have to get home early enough to watch the news on TV, or cook a proper meal for myself. Maybe read a book, like a normal person.

I can't remember the last time I read a book. Surely it wasn't all the way back to when I was a child, trying to manoeuvre through the *Lord of the Rings* in the library that day. Surely not…

God. I need to get home and get at least a little bit of sleep. Even filled with nightmares, some sleep is better than none.

I lock up the office and head downstairs and out of the building into the cool night air. I love the balminess of summer, but I have always preferred the cooler weather. Perhaps that is due to my banshee blood, with its roots in the Winter Court.

I raise my face and close my eyes, breathing in deep. Despite the city environment, Melbourne is still relatively pollution-free in comparison with many other parts of the world. There are myriad gardens around the city, and the bay, of course. Our office near the Docklands ensures a fresh water breeze, no matter what time of day or night. I love the cold bite of air on my skin, after a day spent hunched over the desk indoors.

A sound to my left has my eyes popping open and I swivel, looking for the source. What *was* that? It sounded like a low growl, and not from anyone's pet dog, either.

The shadows morph into solidity as something spindly launches out of nowhere and knocks me sideways. I stagger and fall, my hand going to the pistol on my left hip even as I land awkwardly on my right side. The air whooshes out of my lungs and I instinctively roll. A set of teeth snap shut right where my head was a moment earlier.

Jesus, fuck. What is this creature? It looks like a mix between human and skeleton. How does it have so much strength? I launch upward from the ground onto my feet and crouch, facing it. An abomination?

It grins, displaying yellowed incisors, and the red eyes flare as it licks its lips.

A vampire. Only, not an ordinary one, if there is ever such a thing. No, this one has murder in its eyes, and death on its mind. And it isn't about to take no for an answer.

"Smell. Good. Hybrid," the creature says.

It sniffs the air and wipes a hand across its face.

Spittle drips from one of the incisors and slowly stretches down before plopping to the ground.

I suppress a shudder.

"Yep, that's me," I answer, trying to hide the tremor in my voice. "Delicious hybrid blood. Why don't you come get me, vamp?"

I gesture with the gun, inviting the creature in close, and its eyes follow my movements. The click of the lever on the side of the gun echoes in the night. I have just switched from standard to exploding bullets. Silver bullets, encased in an iron-lead mix, and at its core a tiny sliver of hawthorn wood specially treated to allow it to survive the heat of an explosion.

SUDAP is the only organization in Australia authorized to use the triple-ex brand, and it has saved me on more than one occasion.

I hope the vamp knows what that clicking sound means. I hope it begins to feel something of the fear that is coursing through my own veins at the prospect of violent death.

Which of us will succeed?

"How many have you killed, abomination?" My heart might be pounding super-fast, but I can't afford to show any terror in front of this creature. Fall apart later, I tell myself. Get through this now, and fall apart later.

"Kill. I kill many. Want. Now."

The voice is warped, hardly distinguishable as words, but the intent is clear.

When the vamp launches at me, I shoot at it. The bullet hits the vamp in the throat. Blood, bone, and flesh explode everywhere as the bullet tears its target apart and takes the head right off its shoulders.

The headless body's momentum continues to carry it forward until it lands smack-bang in the middle of my chest. I fall backward, hitting my head on the concrete pavement as the carcass collapses on top of me.

One down, but how many to go? Luc and Tarrien both mentioned the creatures hunt in pairs. So, there is at least one more. The thought flitters into my mind and then out again. A massive headache erupts. I realize I've come down hard on the sidewalk, hitting my head more forcefully than I thought. Am I okay? I feel...weird...dizzy...

Another growl erupts from the shadows, I push aside the dizziness and try to roll out from underneath the headless carcass. Despite its spindly build, I can't move it off me quickly enough to avoid the other loup. I hear the creature's growls increase in volume, and in my disorientated state I tangle in the dead vamp's limbs.

When the second creature emerges into full view I am still struggling to get to my feet. I can't seem to see straight.

The creature stands over me. Not a vamp this time, but instead a huge, misshapen shifter. A bear, perhaps? Hard to tell for sure in its half-form, and with my current double-vision, but the thick patches of fur and the tiny red eyes above a massive snout do not bode well for my future, no matter what type of shifter it is.

I give up trying to scrabble to my feet and instead sit back down on the pavement and aim the gun.

"Silver not kill me. Not fast enough." It grins, a horrible stretched rictus of an expression, and I know it speaks the truth.

In a werebear shifter, silver *will* poison it, eventually, but not quickly enough. Same goes for the exploding bullet. It will do massive damage, but in a shifter this big, not enough, not unless I hit its heart directly. Not when it is already standing over me, ready to attack.

"We take you," it says.

It reaches out its huge hand with massive talon claws and grabs me by the right arm. I try to pull away, but it tugs harder as it lopes away down the street, dragging me along in its wake. I am still holding the gun in my left hand, so I aim at its chest. I blink hard as my head bumps on the pavement and my vision blurs again. Stay strong. Stay awake. Stay with it long enough to kill.

My finger tightens on the trigger, but I never get the chance to finish the job. Instead, the shifter's head suddenly parts company with its body and sails away through the air, disappearing from my view altogether. What the actual...

Rhodri? I catch a glimpse of the prince in full fae

armor, wielding a huge sword that drips with blood. At the same moment, the shifter's dead body crashes down on top of me. My ribs collapse in. I feel a sharp stab and an explosion of pain. Has one of the edges of bone punctured a lung? Breathing becomes difficult. Then impossible. I stop breathing, stop seeing, stop *feeling*, as everything swims into gray and then fades out into darkness.

Chapter Seven

I wake slowly, blinking and stretching and wondering why I feel so rested. I can't remember the last time I had such a good night's sleep.

Wait.

The abominations. The city street...

Memory rushes back in and my eyes pop open as I sit up in a rush, staring wildly around the room. I'm in my own bed. How did I get here?

I put a hand to the back of my head, feeling for lumps or blood, or even any tenderness, but it all feels perfectly normal. As do my ribs. I take a tentative breath in, checking for pain or discomfort from broken bones and puncture wounds, but everything seems to be working as it should.

Did the attack actually happen? It felt so real. Surely, it couldn't have been a nightmare?

From behind the screen that separates my bed

from the rest of the studio apartment, a throat clears. I jump out of bed.

"You're awake." The deep voice is full of relief.

Rhodri.

"How long did I sleep?" I fold back the screen, expecting the fae prince, only to find my apartment full of people.

I take a step back, then look down to make sure I am actually properly clothed. Might not be my Sunday best, but at least all the essential bits are covered with a tee-shirt and fleecy leggings. Not what I was wearing when I left work. I hope it was Rhodri who changed me. Out of all of them in the room, he's the only one who has seen me naked.

I stare around at the group, mentally identifying them all without needing introductions.

"Rhodri, Tarrien. And, Luc." I turn to the two women among the group, perched together on my sofa. Two women who look so much like me that there's no question as to who they must be. Unless, of course, these are other half-siblings I haven't yet heard of. "I assume you two must be Indigo and Aleah?"

The one wearing a slinky black dress, high heeled sandals, and bright red lipstick lifts her hand. "Indie. Pleased to meet you in person at last, Maewen."

I nod, wishing I at least had shoes on. Everything about Indie is perfection personified, from the top of her flowing dark hair down to her red-painted toenails.

"And of course, that makes me Aleah."

The other one has no make-up on, and a slightly softer look about her than Indie. She is wearing jeans and a tee-shirt and casual boots. She sports a shy smile. I feel slightly less intimidated by my country-dwelling relative.

She steps forward and extends a hand. "Nice to meet you, sis."

Sis? Feeling dazed and confused, I take Aleah's hand and shake. It is quite disconcerting to look into the face of someone who resembles your own reflection.

Make that two "someones". I slant another glance at Indie and find her studying me with undisguised curiosity. The three of us could easily pass for triplets, though I know from my phone discussion with Indie that she is the oldest at thirty-one, followed by me at thirty, and then Aleah is the baby of us all at twenty-nine.

Mother didn't muck around in popping us all out one after the other. Not for the first time, I wonder why the banshee Renna felt the need to create so many of us. Along with that is the underlying question as to why she never bothered to stick around and raise us. She visited me once, when I was young, but that was the extent of her parenting. That, however, is a question for another time. Right now, there are more pressing concerns.

"Not wanting to be rude or anything, but someone better explain what's going on. Why are you all hanging out in my apartment watching me sleep? And, for that matter, how the hell did I get here, when last time I was conscious I was trapped beneath a dead headless shifter, wondering if one or both of my lungs had been punctured and whether that, or my head wound, would kill me first? Did one of you magic me better? And were those abominations lying in wait for me, outside work?"

"We think so, boss," Luc Durand says. "I suggest you take a seat. We all have a lot to discuss."

"No shit." I look around. All the available seats are taken. My studio is not designed for this many visitors.

I back up and perch on the edge of the bed.

Rhodri, who has been standing near the now-folded-back screen, shoots me a questioning look and, when I nod, takes a seat beside me. His body warmth instantly comforts me. At least it does, until he opens his mouth.

"Technically we weren't watching you sleep, by the way," he says. "That would be creepy, wouldn't it? We were sitting here waiting for you to wake, but we did put up the screen to give you some privacy in the meantime."

I spear him with a stare. "Great. Thanks for that. Now spill. What is going on?"

Indie crosses one elegant leg over the other. "Rhodri brought you back here after the attack, and called us all. Tarrien used his warrior magic to heal you."

There's a touch of pride in her voice as she states the latter, and I notice she has her fingers entwined with Tarrien who is seated beside her.

Tarrien gives her an indulgent look. "I'm good at that, aren't I? I've done it for all three of you, now."

I manage not to roll my eyes but I notice Luc is not so circumspect as me. The vamp detective and I share a brief grin. The truth is, physically I feel damn good. Better than I have in years, so I guess I'll have to allow Tarrien a bit of self-congratulation because he does appear to deserve it.

"Thank you for healing me, Tarrien," I say. "Good job."

Everyone seems to relax a notch, even Rhodri beside me, and I wonder if I really am so grouchy and unapproachable that they thought I would be mad about being saved from injury and possible death.

Jeez. I know I can be prickly, but I don't think I'm that much of a monster. Am I?

Come to think of it, I owe Rhodri some thanks, too.

"You saved my life, back there with the abominations. No way I could have taken out that were before it got me. Thank you."

Rhodri looks pleased, and a thought occurs to me.

"How did you know I was in trouble? Or was it merely coincidental timing, that you arrived when you did?"

"Ah." Rhodri shrugs as if trying to loosen his shoulder muscles.

The tension in the room notches up.

I narrow my eyes at him. "Well?"

"I...um...well...I planted a tracking mike on your shirt. I was still in Faerie when I heard that thing say it was going to take you."

"You did *what*?"

Luc Durand stands and moves in that fluid way vamps have, closer to Rhodri and me on the bed. "Steady, boss. Remember his action saved your life. He only wants to protect you. We all do."

As fast as my temper flared, it deflates into nothing. Luc is right. And Rhodri looks suitably wary. He knows he crossed a line, there.

"Just ask me next time, okay?" I say.

Luc moves back to squeeze in beside Aleah.

"I will," Rhodri says. "I give you my word, Maewen."

He lays a hand on my thigh as if to confirm his sincerity. I imagine his fingers traipsing their way further up my leg until he reaches my mound and begins to explore more fully. *Stop*, I tell my brain. Stop thinking about *that*, in a room full of people you barely know. Concentrate on what really matters.

I must communicate something of my conflicted thoughts, because Rhodri squeezes my leg briefly and then removes his hand altogether. But the memory of his fingers on my flesh, even through the thick fleece of my track pants, remains for a while.

"After I called Tarrien and brought you back here,

we contacted Luc," Rhodri says. "While Tarrien worked to heal you, Luc arranged for Indie and Aleah to get here, too. It's time we all work together to stop this threat. And we have a way to do that, Mae. Tarrien's dad contacted him again last night."

Now they have my attention.

"You could have led with that!" At their gaping looks, I try to soften my tone. "Okay, I guess you would have, if I'd let you. Tarrien, can you catch me up please? I feel as if you all know more than me at the moment."

I don't like that feeling at all.

Tarrien unclasps his hand from Indie's, and leans forward. "Father wanted to know more about my protection duties, particularly as it pertains to banshee-human hybrids."

My heart thumps hard. The threat is real, particularly for the females in this room, and maybe for other siblings out there I have yet to discover.

"What did you tell him?" I ask.

Tarrien glances at Rhodri before he answers, as if seeking permission to speak. Sometimes I forget that Rho is a royal, and therefore Tarrien's boss. Rhodri gives a tiny nod, and Tarrien continues.

"I told him I had been tasked by the prince to guard all three of you, and it was proving difficult given how different you all are from each other and how you all tend to want to go off on diverse tangents."

I frown. "That's not good. I need him to focus on

me, not..." It seems ridiculous to be shy saying their names. I swallow and finish, "I do not want him focusing on Indie or Aleah."

Indie sits forward. "We're not delicate freaking flowers, Maewen."

Aleah moves on the couch, clearly not to be outdone by her half-sister's attitude. "No, we're not. Indie's right. We're half-banshee. We're stronger than you think. And I want to take down these bastards who killed my dad. And my friends."

Something shifts within me. I'm not the only one of us who has lost people in the past. Of course, I already know that on a rational level, but somehow, Aleah's words reinforce the fact that my losses are not unique.

"You're right. I'm sorry about your dad, Aleah." My voice is gruff. "And your best friend, Indie."

My songstress half-sister mentioned what happened to her friend Sienna when we spoke on the phone. Both women acknowledge my words with a nod.

"We'll stop them," I say in what I hope is an encouraging tone. "One banshee hybrid might be tough, but imagine the three of us working together. There'll be no stopping us."

I don't expect the sense of family that rises within me to be so strong. I haven't experienced "family" for many years. Even back in my teens, when my father was still speaking to me, I had to hide the banshee side of myself because that was the side that meant death. Destruction.

After the library "incident", as he always called it, my dad never wanted to be reminded of the fact that I'm not fully human. He last spoke to me on my eighteenth birthday, when I told him I was about to enlist as a cop. A supernatural cop. He laughed, and then realized I was serious. All the angst and horror that he had obviously been holding in since my birth spewed out of him in rage-filled vitriol.

I will never forget that day as long as I live. It was the day I realized my beloved dad hated my banshee half as much as he loved my human half. The hatred won, and I packed up and left home the following morning.

He has never spoken a word to me since, even though, after several months, I did try to reach out and bridge the gap between us.

Family, to me, means betrayal. Loss. Aloneness.

My dad's rage is one of the key reasons I decided to ignore my fae heritage and concentrate on the human.

I don't expect to look at two almost-strangers on the couch in my tiny lounge room, and feel the welcome connection of blood.

I never thought I would look around a room and see a whole bunch of people who *care*.

Too much is happening, in too short a time frame, to know how to process everything properly. First Rhodri, being there physically when I needed him, and then afterward, offering comfort and warmth when I wasn't looking for any such thing.

Now two of my sisters are sitting on my couch staring at me with matching sets of eager green eyes, determined to help me bring down a bunch of crazed killers. Fear for their safety fills my heart.

And yet, I can also see the strength shining through in their features. *You don't have to always do things alone. Accept their help. Trust that they are up to the task.*

I nod, not hiding my dissatisfaction with the idea but knowing we have a better chance if we work together rather than individually. Maybe that has been the problem, all these years. Everyone going after the bad guys on their own, instead of pooling resources and working together.

"All right," I say. "So, you've told your dear old dad that we're a bunch of diverse creatures, Tarrien. Difficult to manage. What next?"

Rhodri clears his throat. Everyone looks at him. Even that innocuous sound seems regal and demanding of attention, when it comes from the prince's throat.

"Yes?" I ask, when he remains silent.

"Why don't you all go away together? A...sister's retreat, or something. If you want to offer bait, then all three of you in the one place..."

He trails off, but I can't get past his suggestion.

"A sister's retreat?" I don't realize how strangled my voice must sound, until Indie bursts out laughing.

"Jesus, Maewen, don't sound so horrified. I've only just met Aleah, here, too, but we're not so bad, I promise."

My cheeks heat with embarrassment.

"No, it's not that. It's..." How can I explain how awkward I feel? I'm not used to "peopling", other than in a work-related manner. Even my sexual encounters have been brief and impersonal. I just don't do relationships well. And that includes my newly discovered sisters. "Where do people go for a retreat like that? And how would we ensure protection?"

I cannot believe I am asking this. A retreat? Isn't that for entitled rich people who want to commune with nature and eat healthy food, or do yoga?

"What about a spa resort?" Indie taps a long red fingernail against her lips.

Aleah's brows rise.

"You want to go to a spa? With Aleah, and...*me*?" My voice ends on a squeak.

Rhodri begins to chuckle and I reach across and punch him almost-gently in the ribs.

"Ow!" He rubs his side. "I think that's an excellent idea. And I have just the place in mind. We can set up protection there quite easily, ahead of your visit, and it is feasible for the three of you to want to get to know each other, so that might put Targon off the scent, even if he does suspect a trap. Excellent."

Humor lights his features as he smiles at me, and I

narrow my eyes. "You have a human realm spa resort in your repertoire, Rhodri? Interesting."

What fae prince would be familiar with such a place? I *live* here, for God's sake, and I have no idea where the nearest spa might be.

"An acquaintance of mine owns it. A mage by the name of Topaz," he says, and I feel the blood drain out of my cheeks.

No way. No freaking way.

"Are you all right, boss?" Luc asks, frowning at me.

"Yep. All good."

Topaz. Surely, there can't be two witch mages with the same name in the city. I know the witch who sold me the charm is in the healthcare business, but surely not... a spa retreat?

Indie perks up. "Oh, I know of Topaz. She and her cousin run the best spa in the state. It's perfect for...I mean, well..." She falters, blushing, then adds, "I know we'll only be going there under a pretext, to catch a raving lunatic or two, but still..."

She sits back, leaning into Tarrien as if drawing comfort from his proximity.

I wonder what it would be like to know someone else has your total support in that way? I'm tempted to lean sideways, into Rhodri, just to test things out, but I resist the urge. We had sex *once*. And I used him, to assuage a need. What we have—or had—is nothing like what Tarrien and Indie obviously share. Nor what Aleah and Luc have. I intercept a loving glance between my vamp team member and my youngest half-sister, and a pang of envy shards my chest.

Rhodri suddenly stands and begins to pace the small room. "I spoke with Father about raising the whole winter army, should I need it. And in this case, I think we do. Might be overkill, but the more manpower we have at our disposal in this operation, the better. Tarrien, you should let slip to your father that the girls are going to the retreat. I'll give you the address details later. Even if he suspects you're trying to manipulate him, surely he'll take the bait, if banshee blood really is as powerful as they say."

He stops pacing and clenches his hands by his side.

"My mother will likely stop at nothing, if she thinks she can access the power she needs to let chaos reign and cause the Accord to fail. This will work. I'm sure of it." His shoulders roll back and his chin comes up. "I won't let her get away with it any longer."

For the first time, I see how much this whole thing is affecting Rhodri. I've been so focused on trying to figure out how to stop Rhiannon and her supporters, I haven't considered the fact that it is actually his mother in the lead on this carnage. How must it feel, to know the woman who gave him life, is so focused on taking it away from everyone else?

I stand too, and stretch. "I don't mean to be rude, but can everyone please leave, now?"

It's too much. I need some space to consider everything, and with all of them crowding me, it feels as if I cannot breathe. I don't want to be bad-mannered, but I can't do this a moment longer, tonight.

"Tarrien, you speak with your dad, if you can," I say. "And Rhodri can arrange the spa visit. We can all reconvene on bait day, with Rhodri's winter army, and my team, in place ready to pounce."

Bait day. My heart speeds up at the thought of it.

Luc and Aleah rise together and move toward the front door of the apartment. Tarrien and Indie link arms as he reaches for his ring. Rhodri starts to do the same, but I stay him with a tiny gesture.

I need to speak to him without the others around.

When everyone else is gone, I take a deep breath in and let it out slowly. Amazing how much freer I suddenly feel, when my own apartment is not filled with a bunch of people I hardly know. Rhodri watches me carefully, a brow rising as I gesture at the now-vacant couch.

"Do you want to know more about the spa resort, Maewen? Are you wondering how I know the witch who runs it?"

"No, not at all." What a lie. We both know it. I huff out a breath. "Well, yes, actually. That wasn't why I asked you to remain, but...yes."

I shrug, unable to explain why a spark of jealousy flares within me. He owes me nothing. But the thought of the remarkably attractive Topaz, coupling with Rhodri...

I clear my throat. "You said, Topaz? Is she someone you...uh..."

He stares intently at me, which makes meeting his gaze even harder. "She is not one of my lovers, Maewen."

"Oh, okay."

"Nor do I wish her to be. She is someone who reached out to the Winter Court, many years ago now, for assistance with a...personal matter. She owes Winter Faerie a debt, and now it is time for us to collect."

Interest piques in me. The mage I know from the shop in the city always seems so calm and collected. I can't imagine her having any sort of personal issue or crisis that would require incurring a debt from Faerie. If there's one thing I know about the fae, it is that you do not want to ever be in a situation where they hold a debt over your head.

"Does she, by any chance, own a spell shop, here in town?"

I ask the question nonchalantly, but Rhodri's eyes narrow.

"Yes, she does. She lives and works in the city. Her spa up in the mountains is actually run by a manager. Her cousin, Amethyst." His gaze drops to the ring I'm twirling on my little finger. "Topaz?"

I slowly nod. How many witches of that name could there be in the city? How many would run a spell shop and sell charms?

His brows rise. "Small world."

"It is indeed."

A short silence ensues, before he asks, "Is that all you wanted to know?"

"Ah. No." I take a seat on the couch and pat the cushion beside me, waiting for him to comply before I continue.

I swallow hard. "I wanted to apologize properly for the other night. You know. The, ah, sex thing." I'm blushing. I can feel the heat, but I have to say this. "It was wrong of me to take advantage of you in that way. I shouldn't have—"

"Wait." He holds up a hand. "Take advantage? *You*, take advantage of *me*? Don't be ridiculous, Maewen, you did nothing of the kind. I admit, I was somewhat surprised when the evening became something other than what I expected when I ported in to rescue you."

I start to interject, but he waggles his hand side to side.

"I know, you didn't need rescuing, but I didn't know that at the time. It was my choice whether or not to accept what you were offering, and believe me, Mae, I did not wish to say no. Yes, it was unexpected, and perhaps a little more rushed than what I'd like, but it was not something I regret at all. Do you? Regret it?"

His sudden question, and the accompanying steady regard, throws me off balance. *Do* I regret what happened? I can't in all honesty say that I do.

I shake my head, looking down at the floor. My

sudden shyness in his presence annoys me, but I can't seem to control my reactions as well as I would like whenever he's around.

"I don't regret it." I speak so quietly my voice is almost a whisper.

He leans toward me and chucks me under the chin, forcing my gaze up to meet his. "I am very glad to hear that, Inspector Maewen Jones. I would very much like to revisit what we did, only next time, I intend to take things much more slowly."

My breath hitches in my throat. His eyes are pools of blue, no longer icy but very warm indeed. "Slowly? I...think I'd like that, Rho."

I only hope we will both live long enough to have the chance to explore what "taking it slow" actually means.

Chapter Eight

"Good." He bends his head and his mouth claims mine in a kiss that starts out feather-light and builds to a more insistent pressure. Tremors rush through my belly and center down below, between my legs. His lips dance across mine, until I part my mouth and let him in. I don't know why this feels so right, but it does. I want more of the royal fae prince. So much more, and yet, there is so little time for any of it.

His groan ratchets up my need to an even greater level, and a matching moan leaves my throat. Somehow, we have ended up lying back, our limbs half-tangled on the couch amongst the cushions, and when I shift, his erection presses insistently against the softness of my abdomen, ensuring I am fully aware of the extent of his need. His need matches my own. Desire pools in all the right places and shivers traverse my skin where his fingers touch and caress.

"I want you, Maewen, but not here, and not like this. I want to ravish you properly, in my bed, in Faerie."

"A bed fit for a prince?" I joke, because part of me doesn't want him to stop what he's doing. And part of me is revelling in his words. *I want you, Maewen.*

He laughs gently, the sound rippling through me. "A bed fit for a supernatural police inspector. A sexy, intriguing, prickly police inspector who deserves to be completely seduced by her prince."

Oh, God.

"I want you, too," I add, a little belatedly, but surely he can already sense that, given the burgeoning nipples in my breasts that are rubbing against him, and the damp heat between my thighs where one of his legs presses insistently against my mound.

My verbal offering sounds so inconsequential against his, but hopefully he can glean how much need he creates within me.

He raises himself up on one elbow and cups my cheek with his other hand. Laughter fills his eyes and lifts the corners of his mouth. "Ever the romantic, eh, Maewen?"

He leans down and presses a kiss to the tip of my nose. I arch up, trying to regain his lips, but he dodges away.

"No more tonight," he says. "When the operation is over, and my mother has been stopped, I will take you back to Faerie and show you what I mean by slow and seductive. Would you like that?"

Would I like that? Of course, I would like that. I never thought in a million years that I would want to visit the place my mother hails from, nor anticipate being seduced by a sexy fae royal, but here we are. Life truly does move in mysterious ways.

"I would like that very much indeed, Rho."

His satisfied grin speaks volumes, but then he slides off the couch and stands, leaving me faintly bereft. I like my own company, in general. I've never felt a compulsion to be with someone else so strongly. Until now.

"You can stay if you wish," I don't hide the hopeful note in my voice.

His smile this time is regretful. "No, my beautiful banshee. I have much to organize, to be ready for bait day."

Bait day. That term again. It brings back everything that happened earlier, and I sit up and run a hand through my hair, pushing it back away from my face. "I'm so sorry it turned out to be your mother, Rho. You know what it will likely mean, when..."

I don't need to finish. He knows that this can only end in death, for the perpetrators. Of course, he does.

"I know. She cannot be allowed to continue. If it comes down to it, I will wield the blow, to save others..." He shudders, and I jump to my feet and pull him into my embrace.

He wraps his arms around me in return, and we stand in silence for several moments, somehow drawing comfort from one another.

The calm before the storm.

"Farewell, my banshee. See you soon." He kisses the top of my head and steps back out of my embrace. "There are protections on your apartment. You can relax here. No one will get in without a whole bevy of warriors turning up within seconds."

Without waiting for my response, he casts a portal and disappears in a flash of silver light.

It is only after he's gone that I realize he kept calling me banshee—*his* banshee—and instead of being annoyed by that, I actually like it.

I HAVE NEVER FELT MORE ridiculous in my life. Oh wait, there was that one time I went undercover as a prostitute, when I had to wear a super-short skirt and high heels, and so much make-up I didn't recognize the woman in the mirror when I was ready for the assignment.

Other than that time, I don't believe I've ever felt more like a fish out of water than right now, walking into the fancy reception area of a luxury spa resort, arm in arm with two women who share my blood, but who I barely know at all.

"Relax, Mae, we don't bite," Indie murmurs in my ear.

Aleah just pats my arm on the other side.

I release a long sigh. "I know. I'm just worried about... well, everything. Keeping you guys safe, making sure we lure them out, catching them... I mean, what if he clocked that Tarrien is trying to play him? What if they don't take the bait at all?"

I break off, then realize something. "You called me Mae."

"Oh." Indie stops, forcing all of us to stop with her. "Do you not like that? It just slipped out by accident."

She seems as unsure as I am about this strange sisterly relationship. We've all been thrust into this situation whether we like it or not, and the only one who seems at all calm about it is Aleah. Maybe it's all that clean country living out there in Hatton Grove. She's not as strung out and running on nerves and adrenalin.

Then again, she did face down two abominations with only a stick and a little silver knife, so she can't be as laid back as she seems.

"My dad used to call me Mae," I admit to Indie, before adding, "I don't mind if you call me that. Or you, Aleah. I kind of...like it."

Aleah pats me again, and then unlinks her arm from mine and steps forward to the registration desk. She rings the bell for service, and then turns back to us.

"Try not to worry so much, Mae." Her smile is genuine and wide. "Luc and Tarrien know what they're doing. Rhodri, too, I believe. He seems...nice."

There's a wealth of question in that last sentence, but I don't have any answers for her. I'm attracted to Rhodri, without a doubt. Physically, his body sings to mine in a way I haven't ever experienced before. I can't see how we will ever have something long-term, given he is destined one day to rule Winter Faerie and my life is firmly seated here in the human world. And yet, he isn't what I expected when he first materialized in front of me only a few short days ago, and I'm still trying to figure out how to deal with the emotions he evokes when I'm around him.

Aleah is correct. He does seem nice. Remarkably so, given his mum is a complete nutter who is going around killing people left, right, and center, and his dad, from the sounds of it, doesn't have the balls to lead.

I smile awkwardly at the banshee girls, and then the moment passes as the reception staff arrive to take our registration details.

The resort is situated on the outskirts of Melbourne, in the low mountain range to the east. A large sweeping driveway lined with tall eucalypt trees and smaller tree ferns, leads to a large manor-style house with a grand pillared entrance. The reception area is instantly soothing, with piped music playing gently in the background and muted lighting creating an ambience that oozes relaxation.

I had no idea the mage who runs the humble little shop in the city where I got my charmed ring also owns such a luxurious enterprise. Or perhaps, the shop is the side business and this majestic place is the main attraction.

I will have to pay more attention to Topaz, next time I drop in to recharge my opal charm.

Indie, Aleah, and I are all staying overnight in the same suite. It's one of the things I absolutely insisted on. We do this together, we stay together, and none of us branch off and make ourselves an easy individual target. We might be dangling bait in order to catch a very big fish or two, but this bait is alive and kicking and determined to fight back as hard as we possibly can.

"Oh, you've chosen the Deluxe Pamper package with the Magical Booster. And, to start, a mani-pedi. What a delight for you all." The receptionist beams at us. "You're going to leave here so relaxed you won't know what to do with all that joy. You will love it, I promise. Your first treatment starts in an hour—just enough time to settle in to your suite and sample the wine and chocolates we've laid out for you. Enjoy your stay, and please don't hesitate to call reception should you need anything at all."

The woman clearly has no idea why we are really here. I'm aware that, after Rhodri arranged things with

Topaz and her cousin Amethyst, the latter briefed a select handful of her staff. She had to, in order to allow my team to step in and ready themselves undercover as staff members. I made the decision to remove most civilians from the scene, so, apart from a small handful of genuine staff mixed in with SUDAP members, the only customers at the moment are the three of us, plus a couple of female SUDAP staff who volunteered—rather eagerly, I might add—for the task.

Rhodri's warriors will be on hand, too, although they will remain hidden until needed. An on-call magical army, so to speak.

The prince himself is shadowing a member of my team. He made that fact non-negotiable, and as much as his assumption of being in charge annoys me, I'm grateful for the extra set of hands.

I was concerned at first that Rho's presence would jeopardize things, given how well-known he is to all winter fae, and obviously, to his own mother. A glamor apparently won't work either, not on his mother. But, given it is now common knowledge that Tarrien is working under his command to try and keep the banshee-hybrids safe, it doesn't seem out of character for Rho to actually be here, after all.

We have prepared as much as we can. There are plain-clothes police officers stationed outside and in the facility. Though I've never met the queen nor Tarrien's father, others have provided detailed information about the extent of their powers, and Rho cast an image so we would all know exactly what they look like.

I'm concerned in particular about Indie. When she saw the image Rho cast, she developed a fit of the shakes. She gives the impression of having a tough exterior, but she must have been through hell when she was captured and held by the queen.

Her experiences at the hands of Rhiannon and Targon are nothing short of horrific. The fact that she is here today, supporting this operation and allowing herself to be used as bait alongside Aleah and me, is testament to an inner strength that is admirable.

I have never reached out to try and find any of my siblings, and until now, I never questioned that decision within myself. I've done everything in my power to tamp the fae side of my heritage down. *Banshee*, in my mind, has always equated to violence, and destruction. Death. I wanted nothing to do with that.

Now, studying Aleah as she accepts our room key from the receptionist, and noting the determined set of Indie's features as she picks up her overnight bag from where she had placed it beside her feet while we waited, I realize I may have been a bit hasty.

A rush of something fills me. It is not affection, but perhaps it could be termed as a burgeoning *like* for the two of them. I am interested to get to know these women better. I want to understand who they are and where they came from. Even if that means facing what I've always avoided before—my own past.

Indie and Aleah are banshee, but they are also human, and they have both found a way to deal with their hybrid heritage without letting it destroy them. Is it possible, that I might be able to do the same?

The receptionist directs us through an archway toward a set of elevators. We are staying on the second floor, chosen because it will be close enough to ground level for someone with supernatural strength to climb easily, if they want to come after us.

They just won't be expecting what awaits them, inside the room.

Sheer decadence greets us as we enter. My eyes boggle a bit as I stare around the room. The lounge area is bigger than my whole apartment, and I shuck off my shoes just inside the door and sink my toes into the softest carpet I've ever experienced.

"Wow," Aleah says, her mouth hanging open.

"Fuck me," Indie adds, and at that we all burst into fits of laughter.

I can't believe I'm standing here giggling like a schoolgirl, but it feels...nice.

"I'm a bit scared to put my scummy old things down amongst all this magnificence," I admit. "I guess there must be a lot of money in magical witchy day spas."

Crystal chandeliers hang from the ceiling at strategic points throughout the space, and the walls are adorned with a textured wallpaper in soothing grays, blues, and creams that perfectly match the pale gray carpet. The blue stripe in the pattern reminds me of Rhodri's eyes. I shove that thought aside.

"I have been here once before," Indie says. "But only for a treatment, not to stay over. It was a birthday gift from my assistant, Dreya. As far as I'm aware, the treatment rooms are all on the ground floor. I never ventured up here."

We advance into the suite and explore, each of us claiming one of the three bedrooms for ourselves, and then reconvening in the lounge area. We sit on a large cream sofa in front of a glass coffee table laden with wine in an ice bucket, fluted glasses, and a platter heaped high with delicious sweet treats.

"When they said chocolates and wine, I didn't quite imagine that." Aleah stares at the platter.

"Me either," Indie says. "I assumed a peppermint chocolate on our pillow."

Which reminds me...

"Bedroom doors stay open tonight," I say, and the other two nod.

"Damn straight. No way I'm being dragged off by that evil bitch queen again," Indie says.

Aleah frowns. "We want them to come for us, I get that. But what if...well, in my experience those abominations are pretty quick. Will your team be able to get in here in time, Mae?"

I smile reassuringly, though on the inside I'm just as nervous as she sounds.

"We're well protected. Rhodri has his warriors standing by in some folded pocket of reality or something. I don't quite know how it works, but they are very close, and ready. He gave me this"—I lift my hand and show off yet another ring that almost matches the opal charm—"and I just need to twist it and call him. He'll be here almost instantly. My own team are dotted throughout the facility as well. There's no way of knowing exactly how or where an attack might eventuate, so we decided my team would be on lookout duty and Rhodri will bring in the heavy hitters if we need them."

I can't actually believe we're going ahead with this at all, but the case has been bubbling along for as long as I can remember and at this point, I'm willing to try almost anything to bring it to a head.

"Plus, we have our fae protective suits," I say. "Which reminds me, we should probably don those now."

Rhodri provided us with three almost-transparent body suits that are gossamer-thin, practically invisible to the human eye. But he said they are made of extremely fine chain mail that will afford some protection for my sisters and me when we wear them. They cover our neck and torso, and extend down each leg to the knee and down each arm to end around the elbow.

Each suit is fitted with a tracking device, which Rho assures me will work in the unlikely event one of is actually snatched and taken away.

I gave him a look when he mentioned the tracking device, but on reflection I realize it is a good idea.

The more I am drawn in to the ways of the fae, the more I realize how little I actually know. My own fault, for being so obstinate, but as an officer of SUDAP—an organization that deals in supernatural crime—it is an oversight I am going to have to rectify, and soon.

Indie, Aleah, and I retire to our rooms and then re-emerge decked out in the strangely light and airy fae body suits beneath our normal street clothing.

I bend down and touch my toes, and then straighten, jiggling about a little. No restriction in movement, which is great. I only hope they are as effective as Rhodri insists they are.

Aleah still looks worried, and even Indie is chewing all the red lipstick off her bottom lip. I smile encouragingly.

"Let's have some chocolate, girls, and head downstairs for our first treatment," I say. "We need to act as if we really are here for a sisterly get-together, in case anyone is watching and reporting back to Tarrien's dad. So, chocolate first, and then we get to pretty up our toenails."

And then, we wait for the enemy to strike.

Chapter Nine

The Deluxe Package apparently includes a whole range of treatments including massage, facial, and some kind of booster treatment to soften skin, reduce wrinkles, and plump up the lips. But it starts with a pedicure, so the three of us end up sitting in the triple treatment room, wearing white robes over our fae body suits, our bare feet soaking in warm soapy water while three therapists kneel at our feet.

Calming music plays in the background, and the lighting is dim. The whole ambience is one of restfulness. *I could get used to this.*

I've never had a manicure or a pedicure before, so I don't quite know what to expect, but at least the treatment allows me to remain upright and keep my eyes peeled for anything untoward. I don't actually plan to indulge in a massage or a facial, though I haven't told the others, yet. I can't afford to lie down and close my eyes. Instead, I'll keep watch while my sisters enjoy those treats.

I have a gun strapped to my thigh in a small holster beneath my robe. The gun is not the same one I normally carry. This weapon shoots wire netting, the metallic strands treated with the same magic as the special handcuffs. If I tangle someone in this net, they are not getting away easily, supe or no supe.

I also have a small microphone-speaker sitting in my right ear canal, and I can hear the voices of my team as they do sporadic check-ins.

"Western boundary is all clear," says Jock, the Scottish detective who joined us last year. "Heading south now and will check back in ten minutes."

I wait for Sadie, who is patrolling the eastern edge of the property with her partner, but when her voice chimes up, she sounds a little uncertain. "East *looks* clear, but it's hard to say, boss. We're right up next to the forest on this side and there are sections where the fence is not intact. Looks trampled at one point, but there's a tree down right there, so it could just be that."

"Okay." I speak quietly to avoid spooking the others in the room. The inbuilt mike is delicate and conveys my instructions regardless of whether I shout or whisper. "Team Four, head out to the east boundary and assist Sadie in patrols along that side. Keep an eye out for anything else out of the ordinary, and no need to wait for the check in time. If you see something, let me know immediately."

It is unlikely an attack will come via normal human channels, but I have to cover all bases just in case. The most likely scenario is that a necromancer, or perhaps a team of necros, will open up a portal somewhere in the building itself. In some ways, I hope that's what happens, because Amethyst assured us the whole property has been magically alarmed to signal any unwanted intrusion.

The rest of my team pairs check in without incident, and for a few minutes, calmness reigns as the woman kneeling in front of me dries off my feet. She pours a fragrant oil into her palms and begins to massage everything from my calves right down to the tips of my toes and back up again.

I look over at Aleah and Indie ensconced at their respective pedicure stations. Both have their eyes closed and look blissfully happy. Is that what I look like, when I let my guard down? Younger and far less wary.

I feel weird when Indie's eyes pop open and she catches me staring. She winks at me and closes her eyes again. A sense of wellbeing begins to creep over me, and I know that after all this is over, when things begin to calm down, I do want to get to know my half-sisters properly.

There might even be other siblings I could reach out to. Other half-and-half hybrids who are fumbling their way through life trying to convince themselves that family and fae heritage don't matter.

I'm a police officer, after all. It shouldn't be too hard to locate Renna's other children.

Wouldn't it be funny if we all ended up having a massive family get-together at Christmas? *Jeez*. My mind sheers away from the horror of that thought. Baby steps, I remind myself. Start with these two, and see how it goes.

From the delighted moans rising from Indie and Aleah as the therapists knead their feet, I kind of wish we *were* actually here for pleasure instead of business.

Maybe one day, I'll come back here just for fun. Maybe one day, I'll bring Rhodri, and we can stay in one of the luxury suites and enjoy a spa bath together in the decadent marble bathroom.

Who are you kidding? My mind seems to be turning to mush, and all because someone is pampering my feet. Rhodri is a royal prince. His palace in Faerie is probably far grander than anything in the human world. Why would he want to visit a place like this, with me?

I shake my head at the ridiculous nature of my meandering thoughts. Why does Rhodri keep creeping into my mind, when I should be concentrating on the operation? I focus back on the skilled hands of the therapist as she works to turn my feet into things of beauty. A hard task, if ever there was one. Focusing on that, means I am less likely to slip into silly daydreams about a sexy fae prince.

The pedicure takes over an hour. We are down to the last coat of burnt orange-colored nail varnish when a shrieking alarm reverberates through the air. I jolt forward in my seat. The door to the treatment room crashes open as members of SUDAP storm into the space. At the same time, silver light flares everywhere, practically blinding me. I can't keep track as abominations, men in robes, and armored fae materialize from a multitude of portals all over the place.

I jump to my feet and grab a passing pair of SUDAP officers. "Get the therapists out to the safe zone. Now!"

I sprint toward Aleah and Indie, both of whom are already on their feet and backing up to each other until they stand together, facing outward. Sensible move. I join them, and draw the netting gun from my thigh holster.

Noise and movement and yelling surround us, but weirdly, it is as if the three of us are invisible; protected from the rush and the noise by some kind of see-through barrier. I notice Tarrien across the room, staring intently at us without blinking. Is he doing something, to hide us?

"It's a protective bubble," Indie whispers. "Stay close, and stay quiet. Do you remember my apartment, Mae? The abomination attack on the floor above? You were only a few inches from my face, that day in the corridor. Tarrien and I were hidden behind a bubble he created."

"I remember that." I keep my voice low. "I knew there was something—well, someone, I guess—there. I could *feel* your presence. But no matter how hard I tried, I couldn't see anything."

"You were this far from my face." Indie holds her forefinger and thumb about four inches apart."

That close?

"Pretty effective. So, none of them can see us?" I tip my chin slightly toward the fighting all around us.

"Other than Tarrien, no. Not at the moment, anyway. But if Tarrien loses his concentration, then get ready. The protection will fall instantly."

"Can I shoot, if I need to? It won't ricochet?"

"Uh...yeah, uh...actually, not sure on that one," Indie whispers.

I flick the safety back on, not willing to tangle us up accidentally.

While we cower inside the bubble, I assess the room, trying to catalogue what we're up against.

Two black-robed necros stand with their arms outstretched. A pulsating purple bracelet adorns each of them on their left wrists. They appear to be directing magic toward a whole bunch of abominations. Are they piloting the rogues?

I count at least fourteen abominations—a mix of warped-looking vamps and were shifters, though it's hard to be sure of the exact number, with everyone moving so fast. Rhodri flashes in and out of my vision, wielding a sword and a short dagger as ably as his warriors.

For the first time, I begin to see his potential as a future leader. For some reason, I assumed he would stand back and let his men fight for him, but clearly, he's as well-trained as they are, and brave enough to step right in to the fray alongside them. More than that, the twelve silver-armored warriors fighting around him, are looking to Rhodri for direction and following his lead.

It's ridiculous that I feel a sense of pride, watching him in battle. We had one night together, so to imagine anything more between us is just plain stupid.

Both sides seem to be fairly evenly matched, though there are more of them than us. The ex-queen, or Targon, or whoever was directly responsible for sending this contingent to attack us, clearly wasn't messing around this time.

I need to get out there and assist. "Can Tarrien drop the protection for a moment and let me out?"

Aleah shivers against my side.

"Don't, Mae. You have banshee blood, too. Let them..." She trails off, no doubt reading my determination correctly and realizing it is futile to argue.

Indie nods, answering my question. "He can drop it, but the instant he does we'll all be seen."

"Right. So, we need to figure out how to protect you both. Let me think for a second." I calculate how best to proceed. "Okay. Indie, I know you can talk to Tarrien, mind to mind."

Fae who have fallen in love with one another can communicate with their chosen mate without a word being spoken out loud. That was something Renna told me, when I was young. Strangely, I remember the obscure fact now.

"Can you ask him to drop the shield, and let him know I'll jump forward, away from you both? You two link arms and step back, in the opposite direction to me. Tarrien can instantly reform the bubble, and then Indie can talk to him to coordinate while you both slowly move together to a different spot. Got it?"

"No—" Aleah begins, but Indie turns her head to look directly at Tarrien.

"Yes." A moment later, she adds, "Go!"

I leap forward into the melee as shouts go up all over the room. We've been seen.

I can't afford to look back. I have to trust that Tarrien has done what he needs to, and concealed my sisters once again. I head straight toward one of the necros, the one with his back to me as he directs a stream of puppet-like abominations toward the fae fighting around Rhodri. I cock my netting gun and shoot.

Bullseye.

The necromancer screams and falls to the ground

in a tangle of webbed netting, fighting hard but unable to get free. The more he struggles, the more tangled he becomes. Just like that, half the abominations in the room stop what they're doing and shake their heads as if coming out of a dream.

These creatures are still insane, though, and once they realize they are free of the person controlling them, I'm guessing they will start killing with even less purpose and more abandon than before. Sure enough, vicious snarls and growls rise from them.

Rhodri directs his men to re-engage, stabbing and slashing as many of them as they can reach. The other half of the rogues, presumably piloted by the second necromancer, seem to step up the ferocity of their attack in response. A whirlwind of leaping bodies, and flashes of huge teeth and taloned claws fill my vision. Some of them launch at me. I duck and weave, trying to aim the netting gun but unwilling to fire when I might accidentally tangle up one of Rhodri's warriors.

Growls and grunts and screams of pain fill the air, hurting my ears. Then I realize it isn't the sounds of battle that make me want to grit my teeth and cover my ears. Twin wails rising behind me have reached the point where it hurts to listen. I know those wails only too well. I had one myself, once, and hoped never to experience it again.

I whirl as Aleah and Indie become visible. They tumble out of the bubble that had been held steadfast by Tarrien up to that point.

Unfortunately, he is no match for the power of the banshee. Both women fall to the floor, clutching at each other, writhing and sobbing, as creatures die around us.

Damn it. The one contingency I forgot to consider —and the one thing I should have thought of before all else.

The banshee cry.

I feel death weighing on me, so heavy it almost takes my breath away, but the protection provided by the charmed ring holds fast and I manage to remain on my feet.

That is why I cannot give in to my banshee heritage. The writhing women right there on the floor, is concrete evidence that I have made the correct choice to tamp down my power and steer clear of the agony of being half-banshee.

I hurry to the downed necro, kneeling on top of him and reaching into the tangle of netting to find the man's wrist. He tries to bat me away, but I ignore his ineffectual movements. A bracelet, not only imbued with the familiar purple magic but in fact pulsing with a strong purple light. It can't be active within the confines of the spelled netting, but it displays its purple badge regardless.

I sink my hand into the deep sleeve of my robe and use the terry cloth fabric to tug at the piece of jewelry to pull it off him.

The man screams and swipes at my hand. "You

don't understand. You don't know what you're doing. Wait, stop. Please."

To my shock, tears well up in his eyes and tumble down his cheeks.

I harden my heart against his pitiful pleas. "You've killed so many. And now you're crying because I'm going to remove your rotten-at-the-core bracelet? Shut up and let me have it. You're not even controlling them, anymore. The netting is enchanted, and it tamps down all your magic."

I can't believe I'm having this conversation in the middle of what amounts to a battleground. I duck as a vamp launches above me, but its target in this moment is a warrior just beyond where I'm kneeling.

I glare into the necromancer's eyes so he can gauge my sincerity. "Give me your goddamn bracelet, or I'll have one of these warriors cut off your hand, and then I'll take it from you, anyway."

"That would be better. It would be better to lose a hand, than to face death. Only, if you take my hand, leave the bracelet on it."

What?

"She made us! *He* made us! It is not our fault. And if I give it up, the punishment is more severe than you can ever imagine. Take the hand off! Then I won't have relinquished it to you."

A punishment more severe than having half your arm lopped off by an enraged fae warrior?

I give up trying to reason with him and simply

wrestle the band right off his arm. I drop the bracelet into my robe pocket, still reluctant to touch it until we know more about how it works.

His screech becomes a yowl, mingling with the ongoing wail of my two sisters, and I grit my teeth, wondering if my ears will ever recover from this onslaught.

The other necromancer glances across at what I'm doing and his face transforms into a rictus of terror. He does some weird movement with his hands, and the remaining abominations stop mid-battle and gallop over the floor toward him.

I yell a warning to Rhodri, but it's too late. The man opens a portal, and the still-living abominations pile on top of one another into the circle of light. The necro jumps in last, casting one more stricken glance at the man caught in my net, before disappearing altogether.

The sounds of battle vanish almost instantly. Only a few small skirmishes continue, and then every rogue supe still left in the room is dead. The necro in my net is sobbing uncontrollably.

I turn my head and note Indie and Aleah, still on the floor, still squirming, but their movements are less frenzied and the sounds of sobbing and moaning are finally beginning to calm.

Eventually, all is quiet. I stare around, breathing hard, unable to believe that only a few short minutes ago, I was having my toenails painted and my feet massaged, and imagining a sexy spa date with Rhodri.

Carnage is everywhere. Dead bodies, bits of flesh and limbs, and loose heads lying around sporting various terrifying or terrified expressions. Whatever the previous owner was feeling at the moment of death, is still imprinted on each face.

My heart skips a beat when I see a fallen fae warrior, but it is neither Rhodri, nor Tarrien. The prince kneels by the dead man's side and adjusts the man's severed head until it rests approximately where it would be if the man were still alive. It is a small gesture of respect for one of his own.

So many dead. Even these warped creatures were once regular supes, probably just as normal as some of the members of my team. Until somehow, they got caught up in Rhiannon and Targon's twisted little plan and the madness overtook them. In many ways, the abominations are as much a victim in this as the innocent people they have killed over the years.

Luc mentioned his vampire Maker, Veronique, when he first joined our team in SUDAP. She was perfectly normal one day, and then disappeared from their nest, turning up shortly afterward as a crazed abomination who killed Aleah's dad. I can only assume that she was somehow poisoned by Targon and Rhiannon's vile magic, and lost her sanity in the process.

At least we caught one of them alive this time. An abomination pilot. Though by the sound of the necromancer's moaning, he thinks he isn't long for this world.

I ignore the dead for now, and concentrate on the only living prisoner.

I suck in a shocked breath when I look down at him. "Jesus!"

In the few short seconds I was distracted by the carnage, the necromancer has developed a nasty red rash. Some of the bumps have become pustular and are beginning to excrete a smelly fluid. It is as if he has been flayed alive by an invisible whip, allowing a sea of pus within his body to begin to ooze out wherever the skin has split.

Is this the punishment he spoke of? What sort of sick mind would create this for one of their own followers?

I finger the shape of the purple bracelet in my robe pocket, and pity fills my chest. "Where are they?"

"I can't. I can't..."

I squat down in front of him. "Yes, you can."

My tone is gentle and once again tears well in his eyes.

"The punishment for removing the bracelet, is death," he sobs. "You've just killed me, you know. The poison is embedded in us all, and the bracelet holds it at bay. If we do as she commands, we get to live. If we remove the bracelet..."

He curls his legs up into his chest and hugs them, rocking back and forth.

A squelching sound ensues, signaling more of the pus has leached out beneath him.

"You know she is evil, through and through," I say. "Isn't that all the more reason to share what you know before you die? Did you *want* to be bound by this bracelet? Did you *want* to pilot those crazed abominations that kill everything in their path? Is that, truly, what you wanted out of life?"

"No, no," he says. "I never wanted that. I was only drawn in, because..." He breaks off to cough, the sound wet and disgusting. "Because Targon offered a grant at the Necromancer Institute," he continues. "He visited there for a time, to learn something of our magics. Eventually he offered money, and the opportunity to study a whole new area of magic, that of necromancer-fae."

He coughs again to clear the growing gurgle impacting his words. "It sounded perfect. So intriguing. But once I got to his academy—once we all got there—we didn't have a choice. It wasn't an academy at all. It was *her* castle. And Targon said if we didn't wear the bracelet, he would have us pulled apart, limb by limb. We didn't believe him, not in the beginning, but he loves her so much, he will do anything to please her."

"*Her*?" I know who he means, of course, but I want him to confirm it out loud.

"Queen Rhiannon. She's a *monster*! My cousin Jorga said no and tried to walk away, the day Targon took us all to her castle and asked for our assistance. *Asked*? By the gods, what they did to Jorga!"

His whole body trembles, and the pustules are growing. The stench is almost unbearable. I breathe as lightly as I can above him and narrow my gaze, trying to focus on his eyes rather than the stinky pus escaping his body.

"What's your name, necromancer?"

"Davon, ma'am."

I feel a presence beside me and look up to see Rhodri has made his way over to join us. He stands beside me, putting a hand briefly on my shoulder, before squatting down.

"Davon," Rhodri says, his tone as gentle as mine. "What did they do to Jorga?"

The necro begins to sob once again. "They tied him to a tree branch outside the castle. He was just hanging there, bound by the wrists. And then she got a vamp and a were to approach and take his legs. One leg each. They pulled, running in opposite directions. It was awful, so awful..."

Rhodri bows his head, and then stands quickly. When I glance up at him, his jaw is set in a determined cast.

"She, being, Rhiannon?" Rhodri asks in a flat tone.

"Yes. The queen. And Targon, too. He's even worse than her. She's crazy but he's just plain evil. They both stood and laughed while what was left of my cousin dangled there, bleeding to death. Luckily, I think he died of shock before he bled out, soon after his legs came off. Oh, it was awful. They said the next one to say no would be gutted alive instead." He chokes and coughs. "None of us ever said no, after that."

Jesus. I feel physically sick at the images the man's story evokes. What must Rhodri be feeling? And Tarrien, too. This is their *parents* the man is talking about. My parents might have chosen to disengage from me at different points in my life, but I can't imagine what it must be like to know your bloodline is tainted with sheer evil.

I glance again at Rhodri and note the sudden pallor of his face. He looks as if he's about to throw up. He meets my eyes for an instant and then his gaze slides away, the expression becoming shuttered. But I see the flash of horror and guilt before he manages to lock it away.

His shoulders hunch a little and he turns and begins to pace.

My heart twists for him. But I can't think about that now. I nod at some of my team, who are standing to one side awaiting instruction. They jump into action to help me untangle the necro. He is no threat, not anymore. I order them to glove up first, and not to touch the fluid leaching from the man's body. I grab a spare pair of gloves from Jock.

At my order, Davon speaks up. "It's not poisonous. Not to anyone except...me."

I hope he's telling the truth. Even with gloves on, I

almost vomit as I reach through the mess and pull him free. My fingers slip and slide in the goo coming out of his sores and some of the liquid smears on my wrist. It doesn't burn and I feel no tingle, so I assume the magic must be specific to the wearer of the bracelet. Davon coughs again, and suddenly blood mixed with pus dribbles down his chin.

"We'll get you a healer." I look around. "Tarrien?"

At my call, Tarrien hurries forward, his face grim as he stares down at Davon. A tiny shake of Tarrien's head has my eyes widening.

"Oh, but you have to—"

"No healer can help him," Tarrien says. "I am sorry. I would, if I could."

The necromancer seems to know more than me, too.

"Healing was never an option." His voice is a gurgle now, his throat and lungs filling with fluid. "*She* injected her poison into us and then he fastened on our bracelets. He enjoyed it, the bastard."

A coughing fit overtakes him, and a spray of liquid flies out and lands on me and a couple of my team members. I resist the urge to wipe my cheek, and instead peel off my gloves and hold out a hand to the man. It's the only thing I can offer. He clutches onto me as if grateful for the connection.

"I'm sorry, Davon," I say, pity for him growing, even though I know he must be responsible for more deaths than I can imagine. "If you want to make amends, can you not tell us where to find her? Where to find Targon? We can still try and save you…"

He smiles sadly, his teeth red with blood. "She knew about the winter warriors. She made it so we cannot be healed. She…"

He coughs and a fountain of pus spews everywhere.

My stomach rebels, and I focus on not retching.

Rhodri is back at my side.

"Where is she?" He almost hisses the words and I lay my free hand in a cautionary touch on his arm. He takes a deep breath and releases it slowly. "Tell me, Davon. I will avenge you, and all the others. I will avenge your cousin, too."

"Jorga?" The necromancer stares up at Rhodri as if weighing whether or not he is telling the truth.

At last, he nods.

"Badlands," he whispers. "She moved the castle… left only an illusion behind…there's a portal though, from one to the other. In the field…near the entrance to the castle where *she*…was held…"

He nods toward Indie, who is sitting up holding a hand to her mouth. She looks exhausted, and angry, and horrified, all rolled into one. Aleah struggles to sit up, too, clutching her head.

As we all turn and look at them, the two banshees hunch over and once again begin the wail of the dying.

I don't have to look down to know whose death

they are singing in this time. The man gurgles, and then falls silent, his grip on my hand falling away.

We are left with the quiet moans and sobs of two banshees signaling that death has once again visited the room.

Only now, we have the information we need to find and destroy the monsters.

Chapter Ten

RHODRI

ight dead abominations, one necromancer melted into a pus puddle on the floor, and one brave warrior whose body and separated head we will take back to Faerie so that his essence has a greater chance to pass freely to the next life than it would were his remains to stay in the human realm.

My mother's list of horrors grows longer by the moment.

Sickness invades my gut, to the point that I have to concentrate hard not to bring up my breakfast.

My nausea has nothing to do with the smell of the dead necromancer at my feet, though that is bad enough. It has everything to do with knowing my mother—my own flesh and blood—is so sick and twisted that she would laugh while an innocent person is torn to pieces in front of her. Not to mention that she would deliberately poison a whole bunch of innocents to ensure they do her bidding.

My blood. I want to flush out any trace of her from my veins.

But I can't. The only thing I *can* do, is stop her.

The rest of the rogues may think they got away with the other necromancer, but this time, things are different. This time, we know where they went. And we know how to find them.

Maewen directs her team to commence the clean-up, in the way of humankind, arranging for lots of taped off areas, and calling for forensics and photography teams to be contacted.

She gingerly hands over the bracelet to a male police officer, who places it in a plastic bag. She then accepts a new gun and what looks like a double holster from the officer. She speaks quietly with him, gesturing at her sisters. The man nods and walks over to the two banshee women.

Indie and Aleah are clutching one another, quiet now. Is Maewen planning to try and protect them here in the human realm? She must know she cannot do that effectively. Not anymore. The stakes have just been raised, on both sides of the equation.

Mother and Targon will know I'm coming for them.

I move to Mae's side and clear my throat to gain her attention. She turns to face me and her eyes soften with what looks suspiciously like pity.

I clamp down on my emotions, reining everything

in tight. I refuse to let her see *anything* in me, that might lead to pity. I will not tolerate that. Especially not from Mae.

"You and your sisters need to go to the Winter Court." My voice is colder than necessary, but the only way I can contain my feelings is to call on the ice of home. "You won't be safe here—and you can't keep *them* safe, either."

I point to the banshee sisters who are now standing, their arms around each other's waists. "My mother and Targon are banished, which means they cannot cross over from the Badlands on the outskirts of Faerie into Winter Faerie itself. You could all stay with Lady Renna until we catch Rhiannon and Targon. They cannot reach you, in Faerie. I promise."

"You want us all to go stay with my mother? She'd hardly like that, Rhodri, I'm sure." Her tone is incredulous.

"Your mother is... not without her faults," I say. "But she does love her children. She definitely wants you all safe and well, and I have no doubt whatsoever that she will enjoy having you there for a visit."

Maewen stays silent while she removes a small holster from her thigh and hands it off to someone. The action flashes her long legs, and I try not to look. I try not to imagine those long legs wrapped around me. Instead, I focus on the larger holster she fastens around her hips, and the two different guns she inserts in the pockets. The dark leather looks incongruous against her white robe, but also somehow quite sexy.

"Please, Maewen, for your own sake and that of your sisters. Go to Faerie."

I cannot afford to stay here and argue with her. I need to get to the Badlands before my mother and Targon can relocate yet again. Mother might be able to move castles with her magic, but she won't be able to do it instantly.

Aleah approaches us.

"I can get us there, to the Winter Court," she says. "When I was there before, Mother told me how to do it."

"So can I," Indie pipes up, straightening her white robe and strolling over. "I can get us directly in to Tarrien's place. We can contact Renna when we get there."

"Good idea," I say, as Tarrien calls out across the room.

"Do it, Indie, please. All of you."

"Good. That's settled." I turn to Tarrien. "Time's running out. They'll be making plans to move the castle, yet again. We need to make haste."

He nods, grim-faced. He likely feels as sick as me. From the sound of it, his father and my mother are practically interchangeable in their level of evil.

"Agreed, Your Highness," Tarrien says.

"You've been to her original castle in the Badlands before," I say. "Lead the way."

The remaining warriors in the room rally at my side as I mentally communicate with them about where we are heading. An advantage of being a member of the royal family is that winter army warriors are automatically tuned in to my thoughts, whenever I wish them to be.

There are not as many here as I would like, but haste is everything at the moment.

I will call the others forth—those warriors on stand-by at the Winter Court—as soon as I know the exact location of Rhiannon's castle.

One of the warriors lifts our fallen comrade Annerley in his arms. The severed head rests on the body's chest.

"Leafor, you head directly back to the palace," I command. "Take Annerley to the General Council, and explain what has happened. They will know what to do for him, to help his essence pass on. And tell them to reach out to me. We'll need more troops. I will confirm how many once I assess what we're heading into and pinpoint the precise location."

Leafor nods and I lean across and open a portal for him. The rest of us line up, creating a short arch of honor with our swords. Lefor walks beneath the arch, carrying Annerley, and disappears into the light.

"Now, the rest of you, I hope you are ready," I say. "We are going monster-hunting."

I signal to Tarrien, who opens a new portal. We prepare to jump, but Maewen rushes forward.

"Wait. I'm coming with you."

She is still barefoot and dressed only in her robe.

"Definitely not!" I almost growl the words at her. "You need to go to Faerie with your sisters and—"

"Oh, Rhodri. Aren't we over this by now? You might be the almost-boss of the winter fae, but you're not mine. Indie and Aleah will go to Renna. I'm coming with you." She rushes past Tarrien and leaps into the circle of light.

"Maewen, *no!*"

I reach out to her, grabbing her dark hair streaming out behind her, and follow her through to the Badlands.

MAEWEN

I shouldn't have done that, is my first thought when I fall out the other side of whatever we were squeezed through into a snow-covered clearing in a forest.

I especially shouldn't have done that in a robe and bare-ass feet.

"Let go of my hair!" I lunge away from Rhodri and turn on him. "That really fucking hurt!"

"Are you insane?" Rhodri's voice is equally fierce and he glares at me, shaking his fist. "You could have ended up anywhere! If you haven't travelled the faerie paths before, you won't know how they work. You can't just jump in and let the magic gently carry you along to wherever you want to end up. The paths don't work that way!"

Once again, he has a point. Still, my scalp stings where his grip pulled far too hard.

I rub my head. "All right. Well, we're here now. Speaking of..."

I stare around. The atmosphere of the place seems very sad and forsaken. The trees ringing the clearing are leafless, the branches a dull black, as if they died without even having the energy to keel over.

I shiver, and not because of the cold. "Where, exactly, are we? I know you said the Badlands, but where is that? Is it still part of Faerie, but outside the Winter Court? I'm not sure how it all works."

He opens his mouth and takes a deep breath, then releases it slowly, as if trying to control his temper.

"The Badlands exist on the very edge of Faerie. Near the Nothing. These are not called bad lands without reason. You should never—*ever*—travel here alone, Maewen. Fae, and other creatures, often end up here when they have nowhere else to go. And the Nothing?" He shudders. "If you accidentally end up there, you will never return. You will simply blink out of existence."

"Hmm. Sounds like a place to avoid, then."

A strangled groan emerges from Rhodri. "Maewen, you drive me to distraction."

"Sorry," I mutter, and he blinks as if in shock.

"I beg your pardon?"

"You heard, surely. You have fae ears."

"I do. And I did. But I want you to repeat it."

My mouth tightens, but he's right. It was crazy to jump without thinking.

"Sorry," I say again. "But I've been on this case so long I just want to see it through. I want to help."

After a moment he nods. "All right. Just stay close."

"I can do that."

Nothing I can do about my bare feet, though, so I tighten the belt on my robe and double-knot it in place.

Damn, this snow is cold. I wiggle my toes, trying to get circulation into them. My newly orange-painted toenails look weirdly bright against the white ground.

The painful pang that comes with being in contact too long with something cold is already starting up in my feet and I bite my lip to avoid mentioning it. This is your own fault, I remind myself.

I still have my netting gun which has three more rounds. It isn't much of a weapon, but it's better than nothing.

I also have my usual issue pistol with the exploding bullets, thanks to one of my team who handed me the weapon when I was arranging for forensics. I feel much better with that one in hand, though who knows what we're about to face.

Tarrien and the warriors mill around, waiting for Rhodri's lead. He stares across the clearing, toward a building that looks like a small castle. It shimmers weirdly. Almost transparent, but not quite. That would be where they brought Indie, before they held her down and tortured her.

She must have been terrified, even before they took her inside. The atmosphere of this place is dark and forbidding, as if danger is lurking just out of view, ready to pounce on the unsuspecting.

I take a deep breath and let it out slowly, trying to calm my racing pulse. I tune in to Rhodri, who is speaking to his warriors.

"That's an illusion. What did that necromancer say about the portal? Outside the entrance? I guess that means over there somewhere."

He strides off across the field. I'm shocked to see that he leaves no trail of footprints in the snow. None of them do. Instead, they seem to float across the top, moving with a surety that I lack as I stumble after them.

If I'm half winter-fae, surely I should be more in tune with the snow than this? I hope I don't end up being a liability instead of a help.

Halfway across, Rhodri stops and turns. His hands go to his hips as he waits for me to catch up.

My breath puffs out in a cloud of white in front of my face.

"I don't know how you do that," I admit when I reach him, adding when he frowns quizzically, "Run over the top. My feet just sink down into the snow."

"Ah. We're winter fae, Maewen. We're used to it. You would be too, if you chose to accept your banshee heritage."

Well, that explains why I'm struggling. And it is probably a conversation for another day. He seems to agree with my unvoiced thought, shrugging, before studying my attire as if seeing it for the first time.

"I'm going to do something now, and I don't want you to get mad," he says.

I narrow my eyes. "Can't guarantee it. Depends what you do."

"This." He lifts a hand and waves it in an intricate pattern, and my robe unravels and drops away.

"Jesus fucking Chr...*oh*." He hasn't undressed me, as I first thought. Instead, he has *dressed* me, in a pair of tight-fitting black trousers, thick warm boots, and a loose shirt that retains a remarkable amount of my body heat considering its thin fabric. I even have my own neat holster wrapping my hips once again.

"Well. Thank you," I say awkwardly. Everyone else is studiously avoiding looking at me. I flash him a quick grin. "My feet, in particular, thank you."

One of his eyebrows quirks up. "Can't have you holding us up anymore, can we?"

He turns and continues on before I can respond. It is far easier to move through the snow with proper boots on, even though I still can't manage to skim across the surface.

When we near the other side of the clearing, our

party slows. Rhodri paces partway around the perimeter and back, a look of intense concentration on his face. After a minute or two of searching, he halts.

"Here." He gestures at the snow, before using his booted foot to clear a space. It doesn't look any different to me. At least it doesn't, until I squint and focus hard, and finally discern the faintest trace of a warping in the air above the snow. It looks almost like the warping of air when heat rises up from tarmac.

"The portal is here," Rhodri says. "Mother set it in place. I am familiar with her magical trace, which contains elements that are very similar to mine."

As if that last thought is unpalatable, grim darkness descends over his features. The lines on each side of his mouth become more pronounced, and his chin lifts as if about to face a challenge.

He glances around at all of us, his blue eyes icy and pale. "When we travel through this portal, we will find her at the other end. We will find *them*," he corrects, shooting a glance at Tarrien. "I don't know how many of us will survive whatever ensues. You have served our Court well, warriors, over many years. But I will not blame you if you wish to turn back now. This is my fight, not yours, and I will see it through to the end."

"Not going anywhere, Your Highness," one says, and the others all follow suit.

Tarrien just rolls his eyes, and pulls his sword from the scabbard. "Let's do this, sir."

The prince turns that glacial expression my way.

"And *you,* Maewen... I cannot state clearly enough, that I do not wish you to—"

"Enough talk, Your Highness," I say, following the more formal address of the others, but also trying to soften my words with a grin. "As if I'm going to let you leave me in the snow where I might accidentally wander into a place called the Nothing and fall off the edge of existence or something. I'm coming with you. I'm tougher than you think."

He nods. "So be it."

There is one thing I need to do before we enter. Just in case he's right, and one or more of us doesn't come back, there is something I want him to hear. I step up to the prince, resting both of my hands on his muscled forearms.

"You are not like her, Rhodri," I whisper. "No matter what happens, please remember that, my prince. You're a decent man, with inner fortitude you are only just discovering. You'll make a good king, when it's your turn."

His eyes flare with light as he stares down at me. Suddenly, I don't care about the others watching. One or all of us could be dead, shortly. I rise up on my tiptoes and press a gentle kiss to his beautiful mouth. He remains motionless, as if shocked by my action, before returning my kiss briefly and with a wealth of passion.

I wish there was time for more.

More words; more kissing. More everything.

We share a look, a deep look that hints at so much, before I step back and once again pull out my gun.

"Come on, lads. Let's go monster-hunting," I say, repeating Rhodri's earlier words. "Only this time, I promise to hold on to His Royal Highness through the faerie path."

I grab the prince's wrist and feel the skip of his pulse beneath my fingertips before it settles into a strong and steady beat.

Against all the odds, every single one of us enters the portal with at least the semblance of a smile on our lips.

Chapter Eleven

RHODRI

She called me *her prince*.

Heat warms me from the inside out at the touch of her fingers on the skin of my wrist, as we travel through the portal.

I wanted Mae's first time in Winter Faerie to be with me. Though, technically, this is still Faerie, the Badlands is not what I had in mind for her initial experience outside the human realm. I wanted to show her the delights of my home, through my eyes. I love the Winter Court and everything about it, and I wanted to give her the chance to see Faerie in all its beauty. Perhaps then she might understand why I am proud to be the heir to the throne.

Perhaps she would also learn that she does not need to be afraid of her banshee blood.

I have to tamp down my reaction to Maewen for

consideration at a more suitable time, and concentrate on the task ahead.

The faerie path spits us out into an almost identical setting to the one we just left. Only, where the other snowy clearing and grand castle entrance were empty, this one is not.

Armored guards man the entrance to the castle. This one is the real deal; no illusion here. And the moment we arrive, *she* knows. I sense it. That means dear old Mother is still in residence and has not had time to organize her own escape.

At the sight of us, her guards instantly raise their swords and stand to attention, as if waiting for the signal to attack.

My team is still looking to me for leadership. It is a new role for me, and one I don't necessarily want. But I don't have a choice. In the continued absence of the king, who has been unwilling to do anything except mope around the palace for years, someone has to step up and lead these men into what I know will be a vicious battle.

A battle against my own mother.

You're not like her. Mae's words echo in my head. *You have fortitude.*

I wish she had not jumped through the portal from the human realm and had, instead, chosen to hide out in Faerie with her sisters. Instead, we are shoulder to shoulder, about to enter a battle that I never in my wildest nightmares imagined having to face.

If anything happens to Maewen...if Targon or my mother harm her...

Mother, we are coming for you.

The battle cry rages through my veins. *Winter army, hear me. Hear me now.* I call to the troops waiting at the Winter Court. *Gather to me, as fast as you are able. The battle is about to commence.*

The warriors already with me form a half-circle line with all of us facing toward the castle and the guards. Even Maewen, who is not familiar with battle formation, seems to find a spot naturally between two warriors, a couple of places down the line from me.

Mother is here, I tell them.

Maewen turns her head.

"Which means Tarrien's dad is also here," she says.

Everyone gasps, and I blink. "Did I...?"

Did I say that out loud? I mentally ask the team.

I shoot a glance at Tarrien to my left, whose eyebrows are up near his hairline. He shakes his head slowly.

Maewen scowls. "You said it in my head," she answers, and my heart skips a beat and resumes double-time.

You hear me? That's... I don't how to explain it to her. I don't know how to explain it to myself. *Try answering me. With your thoughts.*

Okay, she drawls slowly. *How's this?*

The words reverberate in my head.

Holy winter gods. My mind skitters around what

that means. *We can hear each other. We can communicate, with our thoughts.*

That is not supposed to happen, not unless...

It is pretty weird, she shoots back. *But quite handy.*

Oh, it is more than handy. We can communicate in the way of those who have found love with their mate.

Please be careful, little banshee.

She controls her jerk quickly, but I see it.

You might drive me crazy, I add, *but I couldn't bear it if anything happened to you, my love.*

After a moment her voice drifts into my mind. *You please be careful, too. We have unfinished business, you and me. And I'm determined to see us both come out of this in one piece, so we can explore that unfinished business and see where it leads us. I want that, very much, Rho.*

"Watch out!" Tarrien yells, breaking into the moment.

I instinctively duck sideways as an arrow whizzes past my ear and embeds in the snow behind our hastily formed line.

Then there is no more time to think at all, because Mother's abomination army pours out of the castle gates and is upon us.

The enemy army streams into the field, parting at the end of the small drawbridge so that some of the abominations head left and others right. Before we can do more than reach for our weapons and tighten our own line, we are outnumbered.

I draw my second sword and ready myself to lunge

forward to swipe in both directions at the same time. The rest of our army will be arriving momentarily, I am sure. I open my mouth to give the order to attack, but then tinkling laughter rings out in the cold air and I freeze.

That laugh will haunt me until my death.

Rhiannon.

She appears in the castle entrance, looking just as I remember her, pale-haired and beautiful in a long silver dress. Targon is behind her, remaining a few steps back like a faithful servant. But, even from several meters away, I notice his eyes burn with extreme emotion of some kind. He is not taking his position as her servant well. I wonder if my mother knows how difficult it is to hold a rabid dog on a leash.

If she's not careful, that particular servant could easily become the master.

My mother waves a hand and smiles, as if we have turned up for a social visit.

"Welcome, Rhodri. How nice to see you again. Oh, and look, Targon. Your son is here, too. We were expecting you, of course, but perhaps not quite this soon." Her gaze hardens. "Tell your nice friends to put away their swords, or they will feel the brunt of my anger for their lack of respect."

I'm torn. Part of me wants to leap across the expanse of snow between us, and run my sword right through her evil black heart.

But she's my mother.

She looks and sounds just exactly as she did when I was young.

The line of abominations closes around us and we have no chance to retreat. The only way is forward, into the castle itself.

Lower your weapons, I message the warriors, *but do not let them go.*

After a moment of hesitation, they comply.

Be ready. When she demands we move forward into the castle, which she will, we strike then.

Surreptitiously, I twirl my silver filigree ring, sending a message back to the General Council. *I need my army. Now.* I have no idea if they can hear me from here. For good measure, I send out a call for Lady Renna, too. I know she helped Tarrien find Rhiannon's castle when Indie was being held, so her magic has already proven powerful enough to reach into the Badlands.

Not all fae are created equal, in the magical power stakes. Banshee—at least, full banshee—are one of the most powerful creatures in the Winter Court. I had never met a half-banshee, until Tarrien introduced me to Indigo, and with Maewen using mage magic to reduce her banshee power to negligible levels, there has not yet been a chance to test out the magical reach of a hybrid.

Ensure they send the whole army, Renna. All of them. Every last one. I pray to the winter gods that Maewen's mother hears my message and passes it along to the Council.

"Good boy, Rhodri," Mother says, as my team lowers their swords and daggers all along our line. "Very sensible."

Her gaze alights on Maewen who has not holstered either of her weapons. Mother's mouth parts slightly and her gaze turns greedy. The tip of her tongue flicks out to moisten her lips. "You've brought me a gift. A banshee gift. How thoughtful, son."

Maewen hisses between her teeth.

Don't do anything rash, I plead to her in my mind. *I've called for army support from the Winter Court, but in the meantime, do not anger her.*

Maewen turns her head and looks at me, long and hard. Her voice is silent in my mind. My heart sinks as she swivels back to face Rhiannon.

What the hell is the stubborn woman planning now?

"Technically, *I* brought *him*," Maewen says. "Or my scalp did, anyway. I believe you drained my sister, bitch. Or was that you, Targon? I need to know which one of you to kill first."

Oh, fuck. What is she doing?

Tarrien's father steps forward until he is standing beside Rhiannon. Both of them stare at Maewen as if she's a delicious dinner and they are starving.

Only, Targon's expression is also murderous, and Mother's darkness has risen at Maewen's taunting words. Their hunger is tainted with hatred. I feel it, particularly from her. The darkness in her blood sings to mine. Even though I'm immune from its call—thanks, I guess, to my dad's lineage diluting hers—I'm not immune from its effect. Not entirely.

The heavy darkness weighs on us. It is eagerly watching for the right moment to strike. I take a small step forward in an attempt to shield Maewen from whatever might be coming.

I cannot allow her to be harmed.

Mother turns her gaze on me, and there it is, fully visible. The oily blackness I remember from childhood, normally lurking deep within but now, it has risen to the fore. She tilts her head, studying me, and flicks her gaze back and forth between Maewen and me.

"Well, well," she drawls, and one of her eyebrows arches upward in a parody of delighted surprise. "You found your mate, Rhodri. How lovely. Too bad you chose banshee blood, over that of your own bloodline."

Before I can reply, my army arrives, pouring into the clearing through hundreds of flashing silver portals.

Attack! I give the order and rush toward Mother with a yell that rips out of my lungs.

Shrieks and screams surround me as everyone on the field engages. Clashes of swords, grunts of pain and abomination screeches fill the air. The snow begins to turn red as splashes of blood decorate the previously pristine whiteness.

Mother raises her hands, gathering magic. Targon places a hand on her shoulder, as if providing a boost to whatever she intends to cast.

Maewen lifts both of her guns and shoots. Her net flies true, aiming straight at Rhiannon and Targon, faster even than I can run. Right at the last milli-second, a blast of purple black magic permeates the space around them. The net skitters away and drops to the ground, useless.

I don't pause to see if Mae's other weapon found its mark. I continue my momentum toward Rhiannon. Now I have eyes only for my mother.

My target.

She ducks backward as I swipe with the sword, and then again as I parry, holding off my advance with some kind of protective bubble as she retreats back toward the castle entrance.

Targon is no longer beside her. Out of the corner of my eye I see him clutching his shoulder, bleeding.

Maewen must have got him before he could deflect the shot fully. She and Tarrien run at him, and I leave them to it and turn again to Mother. I slash, and she repels it. I bare my teeth at her, feral-sounding growls emerging from my throat. My heart pounds so fast it almost drowns out the sounds of battle raging around me.

Focus. Kill her. Do not let her get away.

She throws dark magic at me, over and over, in tight balls of oozing blackness. I dodge what comes at me from her outstretched fingers. I continue to slash and parry, pushing forward and forcing her to retreat.

I can't believe I'm in a battle to the death with the woman who birthed me.

Her face is no longer easily recognizable as my mother. Her eyes are mere slits as she concentrates and her mouth is wide and tight as she continues to try and kill me, all the while stumbling back toward the door.

She's not my mother. Not anymore. Continue the attack. She has to be stopped, at any cost.

I growl again and lunge forward. This time, I manage to cut her left hand with the blade. She screams and pulls both hands in to her chest, cradling the bloody fingers.

I raise the sword and clutch tight at the hilt. The only sure way to stop her, is to remove her head from her shoulders. I release a howl of emotion—so many emotions—and swing the blade, hard. No hesitation. There can't be.

Do whatever you have to do, and be a leader.

The blade whistles through the air instead of meeting her flesh.

She's no longer in front of me.

Somehow, Targon reached her first. He is at the door of the castle, still grasping his shoulder, but dragging my mother toward him with a stream of purple-black magic. She disappears through the building entrance in an undignified scrabble of limbs.

But it isn't that sight that stills me.

It is Maewen, floating above Targon's head, writhing desperately and trying to escape the strands of purple that wrap almost every inch of her body.

Fae magic. And necromancer magic. Entwined in the one super-strong, evil strand.

"No!" I scream at the top of my lungs and run at him. He's injured and bleeding. He shouldn't *be* that powerful. Not even with the boosting help of necromancer magic.

The castle door slams shut in my face as I reach it, and I batter the wood with my fists, roaring over and over again as I sense the protective enchantments contained in the timber. No one is breaching the castle any time soon.

He and my mother have Maewen. My destined mate. And stuck out here, I am helpless to do anything about saving her.

Chapter Twelve

MAEWEN

I had some misguided idea that riling up Rhiannon and Targon, and taunting them in that way, would show Rhodri and Tarrien their parents' true nature. I thought that would help the warrior and my prince in their resolve, because I cannot imagine what it must be like to have to steel yourself to kill your own parent.

I underestimated both of these evil monsters, as I suspect we all have, over the years. And now, I am about to pay the price for my own stupidity.

Once the door closes on the battle outside, and Targon continues to drag us down the long hallway into a huge room, the atmosphere becomes eerily calm. Targon still holds me aloft, despite his injury. It was an exploding bullet that hit him in the shoulder; he should have been far more incapacitated than this. I feel the supremacy of his fae magic, intertwined with something more, and realize for the first time why he must have studied the ways of the necromancers.

He is channelling their magical powers, to enhance his own.

And he's doing a damn fine job of it.

I can barely move, though I guess I should be grateful I can still breathe. *For now.* I slide my gaze to Rhodri's mother, who Targon dumps unceremoniously on the floor. She springs up and spends time adjusting her long dress and tossing back her hair. Blood spatters decorate the front of her dress. She cradles an injured hand.

"Never treat me with such disrespect again, Targon." She stalks past him without waiting for a response, and stands beneath me, staring up.

Targon rolls me in the air, right over onto my stomach, so I have no choice but to stare down into Rhiannon's evil face.

"What is your true name, banshee?" She smiles up at me but the darkness dancing behind her eyes is so eager to get out that a shiver runs down my spine.

We're getting straight to it, then. I grin back down at her, even though everything within me is screaming out in terror at what I suspect is coming.

"Mother told me what it was, once," I say. "But I have such a bad memory, you know. I simply can't remember it."

That's a lie, of course. I don't know why I retain the ridiculous name in my memory. Perhaps it was the earnestness of Renna's expression and her serious tone, when she told me my true fae name.

Maewennelechiarien. A name I should never reveal, she said, because it would cause imbalance and disharmony among the two realms I hail from, if I ever provide that information to the wrong person. I can't remember how old I was when she visited and spoke to me—perhaps six or seven—but all these years I've done as she asked and have never revealed the name to anyone.

"Just call me Maewen, like everyone else. Or even better, call me boss."

The queen's smile instantly disappears.

Targon makes a tsking sound. The invisible hand holding me tight squeezes so hard I lose the ability to inhale or exhale.

A strangled moan releases from my lips. He's crushing me. I can feel my bones grinding together. One of my ribs cracks.

Black specks swirl in my vision. When they threaten to take over, and consciousness begins to ebb away, the pressure releases and I gasp in a couple of quick breaths, before wincing at the sharp pain in my chest.

"I'm not giving either of you my name," I manage to grind out. "I'd rather die."

Rhiannon snickers. "Oh, you will, dear. Make no mistake about that. But we can make it much quicker and easier for you, if you cooperate."

Targon huffs out a breath, wincing as he moves his shoulders. Lines of gray-green spread up his neck—poison from the shards of iron in the bullet. I hope he turns to pus like that poor necro, Davon, and dies a hideous death.

"We're wasting time," he says. "She's not going to give us her name. The other one didn't, and this one's even tougher. We don't need it. However, without her name, we do need her blood. All of it. Let's get this done, before we are interrupted."

"Certainly, Targon. It sounds like fun. Shall we do it now?" She acts as if they are about to head out on a date, and as I watch from my dangling position above them, she links her arm through his and they begin to walk across the cavernous room.

"After we drain her and use the blood in our ritual, I will arrange for a healer for you, my love," she croons to him. "Your wound is unpleasant, but it will not be fatal unless we leave the iron in you for longer than we should."

Ritual?

"If I'm going to die anyway, can you at least tell me why?" I say. "What do you need a banshee's blood *for*?"

"Quiet!" Targon snaps, but the queen stops in her tracks.

"Oh, do let's tell her! Bring her down."

Targon glowers at both of us, but he jerks his arm obediently and I tumble down through the air until I hover right in front of them.

"Banshees are rare, dear," Rhiannon says. "Your mother is one of the last of her kind remaining, did you know that?"

She doesn't wait for a response, but continues. "And a banshee's blood is fueled by the power of death. Such a delightful thing to be powered by, don't you think? But it is not enough, for what I want. Banshee hybrids are even better than full banshee. You are half human, and therefore you also hold life in your veins. Lifeblood, and death blood, contained in the one being. What could be more powerful than harnessing that?"

It seems the question is rhetorical, because she continues. "You don't even know what power you hold, my dear. You and your sisters have no idea of the immensity of what runs through your own veins."

Rhiannon's eyes gleam and she reaches up with her uninjured hand and strokes my cheek.

I want to bite her fingers off, but Targon has me bound so tight all I can do is glare at her.

"Vampires know. Oh, not consciously, perhaps, but they know. They are drawn to banshee hybrids more than any other creature. And *I* know. Targon, too. With your full name, we only need a few drops of your blood to enact the ritual. But you refuse to give us your name, so instead, we will take it all. Every last drop."

"What's the ritual?" I hate that I can hear a tremble in my words. I hate even more that they can hear it, too.

She licks her lips, salivating. "We are going to use your blood to bind your power to mine, forever. And in doing so, nothing will stop me retaking the Winter throne. In fact, nothing will stop me from taking over the whole of Faerie. And when I do, the ridiculous Accord will be burnt to ashes in the fires of chaos, and my reign will be unstoppable."

Her voice rises, until she is practically shrieking. Not as effective as a banshee shriek, but the sound still makes me wince. The dark insanity in her eyes is evident, and there is spittle on her lips from the fervor with which she spoke.

I turn my gaze away from her madness toward Targon. His expression is calculating rather than crazy, and in that it is slightly less terrifying to look upon.

"What do you get in all of this?" My question is genuine. I am curious as to why he would put up with this nutter of a woman for so long.

He raises a brow, and in doing so looks more like his son than he has up till this moment.

Before he can answer me, though, Rhiannon says, "Why, he gets to be my consort. The king consort."

Targon looks less than impressed with that suggestion. In fact, he seems far less enamored with her than I expect, for someone who gave up his life and family in Faerie because of an infatuation.

"Let's do this, Rhiannon," he says, in a non-committal tone. "We don't have much time before they figure out how to get past the protections."

Their dynamic is hard to decipher, but I would put money on the fact that somewhere along the way, he fell out of love with her, and instead, fell in love with the desire for more power.

Gut instinct says that, the moment they get my blood, the dynamic will change and he will bind the power to his own magic, rather than hers. Given how powerful he already is, that thought is terrifying.

Does she know that he is likely no longer her minion? Does she realize that he's probably playing her, until he gets what he needs?

My mind races, trying to figure out if I can use that information to my advantage. Can I play them off against one another? Can I cause enough doubt, that they turn on each other, instead of me?

Targon might have me physically immobilized, but I still have my voice to try and throw some shade. As I open my mouth to speak, an idea unfurls in my head.

My voice. What would happen if I were to let loose my banshee power? It wouldn't be anywhere near a match for the enormous magic these two wield—whether together or individually—but if what they say is true, there must be *some* strength in my magic. Plus, they won't be expecting it. The surprise might just be enough to hold them off long enough for Rhodri to break into this fortress-like structure. Even if the tactic is short-lived, a delay of any kind might prove to be the difference between life and death. For me, and for many others.

Rho, I call silently, still unsure how the mind-speak thing works. I hope right now, that he can hear me. *They are taking me to drain my blood. He broke my ribs. There are protections on the entrance, that Targon thinks you'll be able to break through soon.*

We are working on it, Mae. Stay strong. Stay alive. I'm coming for you.

If Targon didn't have me wrapped so tight in the strands of magic, I'd have jumped out of my skin to hear Rhodri's voice actually answering me.

Jesus, you gave me a fright. I'd suggest you hurry. If you can. I'm going to attempt to take off my charm. Release my banshee power. I have no idea what will happen, if I do. Hopefully, it will help.

Oh, gods, Mae. Be careful. I couldn't bear it, if you were hurt, or worse.

I want to laugh and cry at the same time. What a moment to have such a discussion with the person you care about. In my heart of hearts, I don't believe anyone is going to get here in time to save me. I hold back a sob, biting my lip.

And you, Rho. I couldn't bear that, either.

His soft laughter rings through my brain, providing hope where moments earlier I had none.

You even sound begrudging in my head, he says. *But I know you care.*

Of course, I do. I...care...a lot.

My love. After this is over, maybe we can work on your people skills.

I don't take offence. He's trying to make me laugh; I can feel it. Just as I feel his strong need for me filtering through the ether. I try to send the same back, unsure how this extra-sensory thing works, but determined for him to know that there is something strong between us that I wish we'd had more time to explore.

I manage to keep my sobs of pain and fear from leaching out, as my captors exit the cavernous room— I'm guessing it is the equivalent of a Great Hall— through a doorway on the other side.

I bob along behind them like an angry cloud, still held tight by those invisible cords being wielded by Tarrien's dad. As they head up one staircase and down another, and wander along what seems like endless miles of corridor, the queen continues to chatter away to Targon. I'm not sure if she's always like that, or if the joviality is a show for my benefit.

Every so often she glances up at me and smirks, before continuing her inane chat with Targon.

Yep. Definitely a show for an audience of one.

As we approach a large set of double doors in a dingy part of the castle where there are no windows and no light other than what emanates from a couple of wall sconces each side of the door, I feel the faintest slipping of the invisible ropes binding me.

Is Targon distracted? Can I... *no.* When I test the binds, they still hold fast. *Damn it.* But in wriggling, I do manage to position both of my hands together in front of me, rather than clenched by my sides.

I can just touch my charmed opal ring with the fingers of my other hand. *Oh, God.* Do I have the courage to remove it, now that I can? Nausea fills me at the thought of taking it off. I've spent years trying to forget that my banshee half exists at all.

My heart was already beating extra fast with the adrenalin running through my system, but now it feels as if my heart is about to jump out of my chest.

I can't breathe. Or I'm getting too much oxygen. I can't tell which. But I feel dizzy and faint, and at the moment, the binds are not tight enough to be causing that. Neither is the broken rib, which has settled into a dull ache, most likely because I'm not able to move and flare it up.

Get yourself together, I order my recalcitrant brain. *This is not the time for a panic attack.*

Last time I had one of those, was just before I bought the charm and stopped the banshee curse in its tracks.

It's the reason I approached Topaz's shop in the first place, out of desperation to get myself back under control. A police officer having a panic attack every time she heads out on a case is not conducive to moving fast up the career ladder.

You can do this. Just slide the goddamn ring off, and let nature take its course.

We enter through the double doors. There is an altar ahead of us. It is nothing fancy, just a raised slab of stone, but I know this is likely the same chamber in which Indie almost lost her life. Moved from its previous location, but I suspect almost exactly the same, minus the audience of necromancers and abominations she described.

Oh, God. I need to do *something*, or I'm about to be drained, too.

I hold my breath as I slide off the ring and clutch it in my other hand. Power rises up within me. It competes with the mounting panic, until it feels like there's a tsunami tidal wave building, ready to blow.

What the hell is happening? I never felt like this in the past, before I bought the charm. I never felt so much energy—so much *pressure*—as if I have to let it out or risk exploding into a million tiny pieces.

Does it feel like this now, because I'm in another realm for the first time? This isn't quite Faerie, but it's close enough—far closer than anywhere in the human realm. Has my location amplified the effect of my banshee magic?

Or is it simply because I've denied my own nature for so long, that whatever I tamped down, now finally has the chance to be free?

I can't seem to stop whatever it is from welling up and out of me in wave after wave of hot burning energy.

Moans erupt from my mouth, the noises morphing into full-blown sobbing and wailing. I sound as if I've suddenly gone insane. *Have* I gone insane? I am powerless to stop the hideous noises leaching up and out.

Targon and Rhiannon stare at me, their mouths dropping open and their eyes wide. Then Targon's gaze narrows and he tugs on the magic cords wrapping me. I tumble down fast, landing hard on the top of the altar.

The breath whooshes out of me at the impact and pain blooms from the broken ribs, but the wail does not diminish. In fact, it increases in volume. The pain of all the deaths I've been holding inside over the years, comes rushing up and out.

What have I done? I haven't disabled my captors. Instead, I've disabled myself.

Now that I'm out of the binds of Targon's magic, I can't do anything except curl into a ball on my side, drawing my knees up toward my chest and howling as if death itself is upon me.

It is. *This* is death. This is a thousand deaths. Who was I, to think I could control this? I can't control the banshee magic at all.

My nose is wet with snot, my eyes streaming with tears, and the pain almost unhinges me. *It hurts so bad. I can't bear this. I can't.*

My voice rises, piercing in its intensity.

Through my tears I see Rhiannon cover her ears. She backs away with a horrified look on her face.

Targon strains against the sound, his hands

outstretched in a claw-like shape as he tries to direct some kind of repelling magic my way.

But nothing will stop the tsunami of the banshee power that has been held down for twelve long years.

Death is coming.

Eventually, he gives up and backs away, too.

Both turn and run for the door, bursting through and out of my sight. Even though I can no longer see them, I allow my voice to follow them down the halls.

My voice—my inner banshee—finds them, almost at the entrance to the castle. My power does not halt when they do. It continues on, like the tidal wave it is, rolling over the top of them and crushing them down onto the stone floor.

They lay flailing, like tiny beetles helpless against a larger predator.

Death is coming.

The wave of power smashes into the castle doors. The charmed wood is no match for twelve years of pent-up banshee magic. The timber splinters into hundreds of tiny pieces that rain out over a sea of warriors lined up outside.

Countless warriors. A whole army of them. Far more than were there before I was dragged inside.

Winter Faerie came, in support of their leader.

The banshee magic bursts out into the cold winter air, over the warriors' heads, caressing Rhodri at the front of the army, recognizing him as he recognizes me.

My power. My essence. My partner. *We are one, fated and entwined.*

Even without him, I am more than one part. I am two. I am the banshee power that swirls through the air, exultant to be free, and yet I am still the frail human woman writhing on the floor two levels below.

The banshee celebrates life—and death—as the human rocks back and forth, letting the pain roll through her—through *me*—allowing it all out, finally, into the light of day.

Whose death am I calling in, now? Is it mine? Is it theirs? Or is it every one of the deaths I've witnessed as a police officer all these years? Deaths when I did not let out a peep. Deaths, when I held everything deep down inside.

All those people, dying, for whom I never spoke a word. I did not give them a voice. I did not allow this song in celebration of their lives. I did not provide the respect they needed to move on from this life to the next stage of existence.

I am sorry.

I should not have denied you all.

I will not deny you, ever again.

Hear me, now, and rejoice, because death is life. And life is death. And there is nothing in my existence, *but* dying...and I sing for you...for you *all*.

Death.

Death is here.

Chapter Thirteen

RHODRI

Oh, Maewen. I feel you, all around me. You are truly amazing.

I have no time to marvel at what just happened. I will consider it later.

Instead, I put those thoughts out of my head and lead the troops through the destroyed castle entrance, even as pieces of the door continue to rain down on our heads. I come to a stop and stand over Mother, who is still flailing on the floor at my feet with her tame fae-turned-necromancer doing the same thing a couple of meters away.

Is Mae's banshee magic holding them in place?

I lower my sword until the tip rests on the V-shaped indentation at the base of her throat. Out of the corner of my eye, I see Tarrien do the same to his father.

Tendrils of my loose hair flit across my vision and

then fly out behind me, as Maewen's power ebbs and flows, continuing to wash over everyone in the vicinity.

"Rhodri!" Mother shrieks. "Help me up, dearest son. Make her stop."

Around me, my warriors begin to lower their swords, blinking and rubbing their eyes. It is Mother, bending their minds to her will. Darkness dances in the depths of her eyes as she exerts her seductive influence. I close my heart to anything bar the one thing I know I have to do.

"You brought this on yourself, Rhiannon. You unleashed her—you and Targon—when she would never have chosen that voluntarily for herself."

"My son. Forgive me. I am sorry," she cries.

Tears well up and out of her blue eyes; they trickle down her cheeks. But we are of the same blood. She cannot hide from me. She cannot bend my mind to anything other than the truth.

"I see you, Mother. I see *it*. The darkness that lurks within you. It doesn't matter whether or not you try to hide it. It doesn't matter whether everyone else here thinks you're a beautiful helpless angel, because you manipulate their thoughts until they have no free choice in the matter. I see you. You may plead all you wish, but you will not, *ever*, be able to dupe me."

"Oh, son. Surely, you would not kill me? I birthed you. I raised you. We are the same, you and me. Please spare me. Please..."

Her voice is pitiful, and out of the corner of my eye

I see warriors around me drop their swords to the ground and turn away.

She is using her power on them, even lying here on the ground beneath the tip of my sword, and they believe her when she says she is sorry.

There is no one else who can do this. No one, except for me.

My sword wavers.

Maewen's voice rings in my ears. *You are not like her. You were never like her. You are good, and kind, and you are strong enough to do what it takes. Rho, I love you.*

My mother reaches up toward me with the hand I sliced earlier. She has already healed her own fingers from that damage.

"Please," she whispers.

"Mother." My throat is tight with unshed tears. Tears I will not allow to fall. "Goodbye."

"No, son! I—"

I drive the sword deep, cutting off her words, and her eyes go wide as she stares up at me in utter shock.

Did she really think I wouldn't do it? Did she really think me so weak, that I would not do whatever it takes to keep the Winter Court and everyone who calls it home, safe?

As she fades toward unconsciousness, her features twist into pure evil and the miasma of darkness becomes more visible. It coats her skin like a shadow, leaching away any hint of the light. Her lips begin to move within the shadow, casting some kind of black spell, no doubt. I don't let her finish.

I pull my sword free of her throat, and swing hard, severing my mother's head from her shoulders with a clean, two-handed swipe. Then I fall to my knees beside her headless dead body with an agonized cry of sorrow, guilt, and relief.

Shocked silence fills the room as warriors blink and shake their heads, coming out of the trance into which my mother's bewitchment had briefly led them.

"Thank goodness," Targon says, still lying on the floor beneath his son's sword. "You saved me from having to kill the bitch myself. Help me up. The banshee did something to my energy levels when she shot me with that damn lead bullet. I can't seem to rise up from down here on the ground."

I stare at Targon with incredulity, but before I can respond at all, Tarrien swipes his sword quickly, and Targon's head separates from his neck and rolls away along the floor.

For some reason I expect the equivalent of fireworks, but there is nothing. Just deathly silence from my warriors, then a huge gasping sigh from Tarrien. And then I hear the banshee cry.

The dead man's eyes are wide and staring, his

mouth open as if he is just about to speak. But he is clearly as dead as my mother.

I don't wait to gauge Tarrien's reaction. Instead, I follow Maewen's wailing cry, running through the castle until I reach a huge space that looks like a prayer room from the human realm. Pews stretch out in rows in front of a large stone altar.

Atop the altar is Maewen, still writhing in agony and crying as if her heart is truly broken.

I race forward, stowing my sword and dagger as I go, so both hands are free to gently lift her from the stone.

"Ribs," she gasps, as she continues to cry.

I cradle her gently, and use a portal to travel back more quickly to the castle entrance where I find Tarrien staring blankly down at his dead father.

"I need your healing, Tarrien." I glance around at the other warriors. "Or any of you. Quickly please. She's hurt."

At least her sobs are beginning to ease. Death has been and gone, and finally, her crazy banshee power begins to wind itself back to the hybrid body from which it spewed out.

The hybrid body shivering in my arms, from shock and exhaustion and pain.

She hiccups a few times and attempts a laugh, then winces.

"God damn it," she whispers. "Can't believe he got my ribs. Again."

"We will heal you, my love. It won't be long. Tarrien!"

Finally, Tarrien looks up at me, and then notices Maewen tucked into my chest. His expression clears. The winter warrior is back from wherever his grief and guilt took him.

I nod toward his father. "Are you taking his body back, to Faerie? You have my permission to do so, if you wish."

"Are you?"

I don't look at the dead queen. I don't need to. The mother I knew and loved died many years before this. "No. She killed too many."

"I agree. Let them rot here in the Badlands."

He strides over to us, and reaches out to run his hand in the air just above Maewen's curves. I don't want to relinquish her to him. I like the feel of her body warm against mine. It feels right, to hold her.

Perhaps he senses my need, because he makes no move to take her from me.

"Not fatal," he confirms. "But she is in a lot of pain."

"No shit." Maewen's voice is still feeble but her feisty nature is clearly not dulled. "Rho, can you please just take me back to Faerie? The real Faerie—your Winter Court—not this bullshit nowhere bad land. Please?"

Tarrien looks at me in question, and I nod, resisting the urge to squeeze her tight and never let her go.

"My bedroom suite at the palace," I say. "I will meet you there, Tarrien. Be prompt."

"Yes, Sire."

Sire? That form of respectful address is reserved for the king, not for me. I am only the heir apparent.

We exchange a look, one that lets the other know we recognize each other's conflicted emotions over what we've just done to our parents. And then Tarrien does something he has never done before, in front of me. At least, not with the genuine honesty he shows now. He bows. The other warriors all follow suit.

I blink in shock at the sea of armored soldiers all bowing their heads as one. When they rise, I nod my thanks to them all, swallowing down a lump of emotion.

Then I open a portal and step into the light, finally carrying my banshee hybrid home.

MAEWEN

This version of Faerie is a damn sight nicer than the Badlands. It's still crisp-looking and snow-filled outside the glass windows in Rho's suite—I make a mental note to ask him if they ever have spring or summer here in the Winter Court—but the rooms we arrive in through the silver fae paths are cozy and warm.

The only cause to shiver here, is delight at being carried by Rho, and held so close against his manly chest.

There's a large stone fireplace on one side of the room, filled with crackling golden flames that seem to give out comfort as much as heat.

Despite the agonizing pain on every breath, and the sheer exhaustion that sends aches through my whole body, something within me relaxes when I stare into the soothing blaze.

My tranquil state might also have something to do with the steady sound of Rho's heartbeat beneath my ear as I lean against him.

He lowers me gently onto a silver and white coverlet, atop the most comfortable bed I've ever lain on, and then sits beside me. Even the pain of breathing is eased somewhat on this beautiful soft mattress.

I run my hand over the coverlet, so weak from whatever it was that rushed out of me in the castle earlier, that I can barely move. I manage a smile up at the prince when he adjusts my head a little, sliding a pillow underneath and pushing my hair out of my face.

"Advantages of being royal, I suppose," I manage. "You get a damn fine bed to sleep on."

"Well." He lifts a brow in a suggestive manner. "You can try it out too, once Tarrien has healed you. If you want?"

Despite the teasing, there's still a note of

uncertainty in his tone. Neither of us really knows what this thing is, between us. But I do know, after everything that has happened, that life is too short to worry about lost regrets. I'm ready to explore what we have; see where this thing might lead.

I am just about to tell him that, when Tarrien and what seems like a whole army of people pops into the bedroom with us.

In reality, it is only Renna, followed closely by Indie and Aleah, who appear behind Tarrien. Renna steps forward and then halts, as if she wants to approach but isn't quite sure of her welcome.

To be honest, I'm not sure what sort of welcome I want to give her.

I haven't seen her since I was a child, and yet I would know her anywhere. She looks exactly the same. Perhaps even more beautiful than she did back then, if that is possible. Her long hair falls loose down past her shoulders. Her red-painted fingernails tap at her perfectly formed lips, and her green eyes are curious as she studies me.

My half-sisters have no such restraint. They both rush to my side.

"Oh, thank God you're okay," Aleah says.

I can't seem to gather the breath to answer her, but Indie speaks up for me, saying exactly what I would have said, if I could.

"She doesn't exactly look okay, *yet*."

It's still weird, seeing them both together and

knowing how much like me they look and—in Indie's case—even how much they sound like me. But I'm grateful for their presence.

Renna makes a small noise and we all look toward her. She is smiling, with tears brimming now in her eyes. She looks for all the world like a proud and happy parent. Truly, I do not get her at all.

Then Indie speaks again and my attention is drawn away from Renna.

"I'm sure Tarrien will fix you," she says. "Won't you, my love?"

She casts an anxious glance toward her fae warrior lover, who steps up beside me and briefly squeezes Indie's shoulders.

"Of course. But all of you need to leave now," he says. "Go into the sitting room next door and wait for me. Lady Renna, you stay. Your power and mine together will knit her broken bones more successfully. Especially since she shares your blood."

Rho grumbles at being ushered out of his own bedroom chamber, but my sisters grab his hands and pull him along with them, ensuring he complies.

He glances over his shoulder as they exit, and I manage a feeble wave of my fingers.

He grins crookedly at me, and my heart swells. I *definitely* want to explore whatever it is, with him.

Once the others have gone, Renna sits on the bed beside me. "We will fix you, dear daughter. But you need to sleep, while we work. Rest now, and when you wake, you will be whole and pain-free."

"Wait, I've got so many questions. I don't want—"

"Shh. Now look into my eyes, Maewen, and relax."

"Will you help me? Learn how to control my powers so they don't go berserk the way they—"

"Shoosh, child. I will. If you just be quiet, now, and concentrate on my eyes."

I want to ask her why she left us all. I want to ask how she can heal, and whether that is a banshee trait that I might have, too. I want to know how to control the rush of power that erupted from me in the Badlands, and whether there is any way to do that without having to use a mage charm. I want to ask so many things, but I can't seem to stop from staring deep into Renna's emerald gaze, and my eyelids become so heavy, my thoughts jumble into one another, until I cannot think properly.

Darkness descends, and I sleep. And I do not dream at all...

Chapter Fourteen

When I wake, I am pain-free. Nothing hurts. I stretch and smile, keeping my eyes closed for a few moments longer, enjoying the feeling of true warmth and comfort. I feel...fantastic. Like I've been rejuvenated. Like I wasn't broken and achy and...*oh*.

My eyes pop open as memories tumble back in.

I'm still lying in Rhodri's bed.

The prince is curled around me like a large spoon, asleep, if the tiny snore vibrating in my ear is anything to go by. His arm lies heavily across my ribs—obviously now healed because there is no twinge whatsoever beneath the pressure of his limb resting there.

Both of us are naked.

My bottom presses into his groin, skin against skin, and as soon as I realize that, I can't help myself. I wiggle my arse, waking his flesh which responds even before his snore ceases and he groans and stretches behind me.

I turn until we are lying face to face, waiting for him to wake up properly. His features are softer when infused with sleep, the regal and slightly haughty aspect of his personality not in evidence at all.

In this moment, he looks like my idea of the perfect man. Sexy, sleepy, and with an expression of pure delight when he finally opens his eyes fully and sees me staring at him. That look. It warms me all through, from my scalp to my toes.

I return his grin with a tentative one of my own.

"Morning, sleepyhead," I say. "Or, evening, or whatever time it is here in Faerie."

"Morning, I believe," he answers. "Late morning. And I deserve the sleep-in, after waiting up most of the night while Tarrien and Renna healed your broken bones."

"You do." I reach up a hand and smooth back his tangled hair. He turns his head and kisses my palm. Tingles spark from the point of contact. "Thank you for bringing me back here to be fixed. I will have to thank Renna and Tarrien, of course, but I will find them later. Right now..."

I reach with my other hand down beneath the covers, checking to see if his flesh is still as responsive as it was when I had my back to him. It is.

I smile slowly, and explore his erection. That is, until he twists out of my grasp.

"Oh, I'm sorry," I say. "I thought you wanted—"

He grabs both of my wrists and brings them up above my head, pinning me back against the bed. "Make no mistake at all, Mae. I *do* want you. I want you badly. But this time, it is going to be on *my* terms."

My heart jumps in my chest and butterflies swirl in my belly at the throb of passion lacing his words.

"That's good. About ti—"

He doesn't let me finish. Instead, he dips his head and claims my lips in a way that is both forceful, and seductive. He teases an immediate response from me, my mouth opening up to let him in, and the resultant shudder of desire rolls through me like a wave.

I moan, the sound swallowed by him. His erection shifts and hardens even further where it lies trapped between our bodies.

I reach for him but he still has my arms in his grip. The lack of ability to move is nothing like the feeling I had in the Badlands, when I was bound by magic. Now, with Rhodri, I find that I *want* him to control me. No one else has ever had the balls to do that, before now.

He breaks off the kiss and grins at me. "Do you promise to leave your hands where they are right now, if I let go? Or do I need to tie your wrists to the bed head?"

My need intensifies.

"I can't promise," I say, and a peculiar thrill runs through me when he waves a hand and suddenly, I am restrained by the wrists with soft cords that bind me to the bed head rail.

"The advantage of magic. Lesson one," he says, and throws off the bedcovers until my naked body is fully on display. "Beautiful."

He traces an aimless pattern along my collar bone and down, around each of my breasts, causing my nipples to harden into rosy pebbles.

"Are they eager for some attention?" he asks, and blows on each of them first before taking one in his mouth. As he suckles, I feel the same exquisite sensation in the other breast, too. It is as if he is suckling on both my breasts at the same time. The wave is so intense I arch my hips upward and release a throaty groan.

"God, that feels so fucking good, Rho. How are you doing that? Oh, my God, that feels good."

Eventually, he stops and flashes another grin. "Magic advantage. Lesson two."

He shifts lower, pressing a trail of kisses over my abdomen and down to my mound. With my hands bound like this, I can't do anything but lie here and enjoy it. He pushes my legs apart, and traces my seam with his fingers, before dipping in with his tongue.

"Oh, yes!" I arch up into him, my movements frenzied, as his tongue finds and circles my clit.

His mouth is working miracles all on its own, no magical boost required. I want to wait until he's inside me to come, but I don't know if I can. The feeling is so damn good, the sensation of his hot mouth and skilled tongue doing so much down there, that when he slips a finger inside my channel I begin to buck in earnest. My wrists pull vainly against their bindings, the restriction more of an aphrodisiac than I expect.

"I can't hold on, Rho. I can't..."

He lifts his face up, just slightly, and his words breeze over my heated flesh.

"Then come, little banshee," he whispers, blowing on my clit as he works his fingers deep, and I tip over the edge into orgasm with a strangled scream.

I drift, and then finally come back down to find Rho has moved back up to lie beside me. He strokes my face and stares at me with eyes that have no ice left in them whatsoever. Only heat. Brilliant sapphire heat, waiting for his turn to satiate himself.

"Was that lesson number three?" I ask, still breathless.

His eyes crinkle at the corners.

"Oh, no." He moves over me, resting up on his elbows, and encourages my legs to part. Finally, he releases my wrists from their binding. I clutch at his shoulders, ready for whatever comes next. "*This* is lesson three."

He slides into me in one smooth thrust. I wrap my legs around his hips and hold on for the ride as he begins to pump. The slapping sound of flesh on flesh fills the room, and my breathing shortens as desire rises instantly once again. This time, my need is seated deep inside, where the tip of his organ pushes insistently, right at the core of my being.

My moans intensify, mingling with his deep, throaty groans, and then we find ourselves in sync in the age-old rhythm of love that builds to unbearable pressure.

"Mae," he cries out, and then his voice becomes an inarticulate roar. He shudders hard as he comes, and the rush of heat inside me tips me right over the edge once again.

This time the release is even more intense than before. I shake and tremble beneath him as my channel clenches around his flesh in a climax so strong, I almost lose consciousness.

I think I fall asleep. I'm not sure, but after a time I come back to awareness to find Rho watching me.

"Lesson number three was pretty good," I say. "How many more are there?"

He laughs gently. "Oh, I have thousands of lessons, Mae. I could spend many years teaching you."

"Hmm. I might have a few lessons of my own, you know."

"I have no doubt about that, Inspector Maewen Jones. No doubt whatsoever. And I can't wait to try some of them out with you."

As much as I want to continue this enjoyable banter, there are many questions tumbling around in my mind. I sit up and hug my knees to my chest. After a moment of studying my expression, he also sits up.

"What is it, Mae?"

"I like you, Rho. I mean, I really like you."

He nods. *I know, my love. We would not be able to communicate with each other in this way, if we did not have extremely strong feelings for one another.*

The words are in my head. He hasn't spoken out loud.

So, if we can do this—talk with one another like this—then we don't need to even state how we feel? It is simply...fact?

He grunts.

"We can state it if we wish," he answers aloud. "But we do not need to."

I am beginning to care for you a great deal, Inspector Maewen Jones. There. Is that statement enough?

Same, Rho. I'm beginning to care, very much indeed.

"But that leads to my question. I like my job. I like my *life*, Rho. But you...you're a royal fae. You are going to be king one day. Probably one day soon. I don't see how we can make it work, between us." I pick at the bed cover. "Do *you*? I want to. I just...don't know how."

He frowns down at my hand, and reaches out to cover it with his own larger one. "It is true that I will likely step up and lead Winter Faerie. Very soon. That is a discussion I am not looking forward to with Father, but it is inevitable, I think. The Council are already pushing for it, so I know I have their blessing. And deep down, I think Father is ready to step aside. He hinted as much in our last conversation.

"But that shouldn't be an issue, Mae. The fae paths are instant, and I don't see why we can't have two homes. You could work in the human realm, and return home to Faerie more quickly than any standard daily commute in the human world. We could live here in the winter palace, and keep the other place—your home—as our city getaway apartment. I see now how much your police work means to you. I would never ask you to give that up if you didn't wish it."

"Aren't the faerie paths problematic, time-wise? Aleah said the timelines aren't always lined up, between here and the human world."

"As Winter King, I will have the ability to regulate the faerie paths somewhat. I don't believe that will be an issue, now that you have made me aware of it. So, there is no reason we can't make it work, if we both believe in what we have, together."

He finishes with a question in his tone. I consider what he's just said, and realize he's right. Maybe I'm simply throwing up obstacles, because I'm scared of committing to anything that relates to relationships.

"I do believe in it, Rho. I believe in you. In *us*. And I like the idea of a getaway." My lips curve up as I glance at him. "But you know the getaway apartment is going to have to be here, in Faerie. Not the other way around."

He chuckles. "Always contrary, eh? All right. I can accept that. For now."

I lay my head against his muscled upper arm. He

rests his cheek atop my head. It feels so right. Ridiculously so. I never expected to meet anyone I wanted to start a relationship with, let alone someone like the future king of the Winter Court of Faerie.

A cop and a king. From two different worlds. It's insane. And yet, my heart beats faster every time I consider it. I am keen to give *us* a go.

There is something I want to clarify, first. "I need to explain more about why I denied my banshee side for so long."

He moves sharply beneath me, and I lift my head, turning to look into his eyes.

"When my friends died, I was ten. I did nothing for them, except cry and scream and carry on like a, well, like a *banshee*, while a monster tore them apart outside the library. Afterward, everyone fussed over me, and I felt so guilty. As if my two best friends were forgotten, because I screamed more loudly than they did. I made so much noise, it was as if everyone forgot about *them*.

"Ever since that day, I've wanted to give all victims a voice. Give them the chance to speak up, even after death, and ask for justice for whatever wrongs were done to them. By tamping down my own voice—my banshee cry—I felt like there was more chance for the victims to be heard. I wanted to be a good cop. The best I could be. To find the killers of all those victims out there, and to offer respect for the dead. To me, I could only do that, if I shut off my banshee magic."

"I understand, Mae."

"Do you, though? You were so angry, that day, when you found out about my charm."

"I was," he says. "But I got over it. And to be fair, we would never have stopped Rhiannon and Targon if you hadn't unleashed twelve years of banshee power all at once. You unstoppered your magic, and it was only *because* of that pent-up blast, that I was able to do what I had to do, and Tarrien as well. Without you, and your tamped down magic that was finally let loose, more people would undoubtedly now be dead."

I hadn't considered that, but I like his way of thinking.

We make a good team, then, don't we? I grin at him, and he grins happily back.

The best, Mae.

We sit in companionable silence for a minute.

"I'm sorry, about her," I say eventually. "I wish it could have been different, for you and Tarrien."

He shrugs. "It ended as it had to. And to be honest, I lost her long ago. The creature I killed was not her. Not anymore."

Again, silence falls, only this time, the sound of a fire crackling in the grate rises through our quiet musing. It is remarkably cozy here. I will enjoy spending time with Rho, and getting to know his beloved Winter Faerie.

I am even a little bit curious to spend some time with Lady Renna. Dear old mom.

Mae?

Yes, Rho?

I think it might be time for lesson number four.

"Four?" I squeak out loud.

He pushes my shoulder gently, urging me back against the soft pillows. "Lessons four to ten, coming right up."

He wiggles his fingers, his eyes darkening again to a rich sapphire color as he stares down at me, and the feel of several invisible feathers begin to whisper across my skin. The touch is so light and tantalizing that the air whooshes out of my lungs in a rush.

"I definitely like the feel of lesson four," I say, laughing breathlessly.

I can't wait to begin the future with my sexy fae prince. The coming lessons only add to the delightful promise of what we might build, together.

The End

I hope you enjoyed this third instalment in the *Blood Fae Chronicles* series.

There will be more coming soon in the *Blood Fae Chronicles* world, including *Banshee Quest*, Lady Renna's story, plus a whole new trilogy featuring witch-mage Topaz and her cousins, Amethyst and Sapphire.

Want to see where it all began? Read Aleah and Luc's story in

Banshee Cry

Blood Fae Chronicles, book 1

Then read Indigo and Tarrien's story in

Banshee Song

Blood Fae Chronicles, book 2

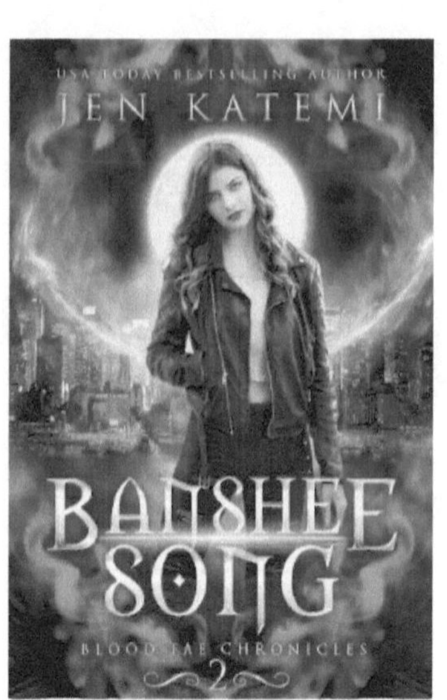

USA TODAY BESTSELLING AUTHOR
JEN KATEMI
BANSHEE SONG
BLOOD FAE CHRONICLES
2

Jen Katemi is a *USA Today* bestselling author of steamy contemporary and paranormal fantasy romance. She is published with Evernight Publishing, and previously as Jennifer Lynne with Red Sage. Jen also has forged a successful indie career starting with her popular BLOOD FAE CHRONICLES, GODS OF LOVE and FORBIDDEN series.

When she's not writing, Jen looks after the family, pampers various cats, and tries to find a smidgen of time for her husband. She lives in Melbourne, Australia.

Read More from Jen Katemi
www.JenKatemi.com/